Dogs and Dragons

Edited by

Joy Ward

Barky Bunch Publishing

Dogs and Dragons

Barky Bunch Publishing

St. Louis, Missouri

www.joyward.net

ISBN:0692561218

Cover by Emily Mottescheard

Dogs and Dragons is dedicated to my sweet Walt and all the dogs who have shared their lives with me starting with Jingle Bells, continuing on with Kreiger, Heidi, Haint, Mishka, Maggie, Solo, Deborah, Missy, Reba, Annie, Saucy, Nigel, Cloudy, Sol, Luna, Rocky, Tank, Midas, Star, Sarge, Beatrice, Daisy, Jersey, Seamus, Toby, Bear, Ned, And all the other furred ones in my life.

All of you have taught me more than I can ever say.

Copyright Acknowledgements

Table of Contents

Maybe being bitten by a werewolf has a bright side if you're the right person.

A Rose is a Rose...

by Joy Ward

Rosie sat staring out her bedroom window at the beautiful day beyond it where she could see the neighborhood girls kicking a soccer ball up and down the soccer field. The window was open so she could hear their excited shouts as the late spring breeze brought in the fresh smells of green grass and early lilacs. The blue gingham curtains fluttered and Rosie could feel the soft blue chenille bedspread under her short, bare legs.

Oh, how she wished she could be out there with them! Rosie loved soccer. She dreamed of being Mia Hamm or one of the other great soccer players she saw on television. She imagined running the ball down the field and, with a well placed kick, scoring a winning goal. How the crowd roared in her day dreams!

But Rosie knew this was just a dream. Rosie knew that being a "little person" meant she could never play soccer on a team, not even a pickup team. Nobody wanted her with her crooked little legs on their team. She could cheer on her friends and wear her favorite players' colors but she would never be a soccer hero.

Everyone liked Rosie. They always welcomed her to their parties. The girls would even braid her long blonde hair at the sleepovers. While the other girls chatted about their games and boyfriends, Rosie sat quietly listening and smiling at whatever was being said around her.

The girls were nice to her, even though she wasn't quite like them. She would never be more than 4 feet tall, if that. At twelve years old Rosie was a little under 3 feet tall. Her stunted, crooked legs would never be the long, lean ones she saw on the soccer players. Her legs hurt after a few hours of walking, forget running up and down a soccer field.

No, Rosie would always be a cheerleader but never a star.

Rosie tried very hard not to feel sorry for herself. After all, she did have loving parents and good friends. But still... A single tear slipped out from her right eye and slid down her perky nose. Her friends would have been surprised to see their normally cheerful friend crying. But once in a while she felt just a little sorry for herself.

Rosie slid off the bed, wiped her face and headed downstairs where her parents and younger brother, Jimmy, waited for her to leave on the annual family camping trip. The gear and luggage stood piled by the front door.

"Oh, there you are, sweetie." Her mother was already tricked out in her camping best of khaki shorts and purple floral camp shirt. Her mother always looked like a model for an upscale catalog. She had been a model before marrying Rosie's father and every hair had to be in place, even when gardening. She never said it but Eosie knew her Rosie's "situation" was a sore point for her mother. She tried to dress Rosie to hide her crooked legs that were so much the opposite of her mother's long, thin ones. "I was just about to send Jimmy up for you."

Jimmy was pawing through his backpack when he looked up and stuck out his tongue at Rosie. "Yeah, I told Mom we should leave you home."

"Jimmy, shame on you!" Their mother reached across and swatted his Redbirds baseball cap off his head. She turned back to her daughter. "Rosie, do you have everything you need?"

Rosie kept her tear-stained face out of the sunlight so her mother would not get upset. Rosie was the only "little person" in her family and was very aware that her mother felt guilty about her daughter's situation. The doctors never found a reason for Rosie's size. She fought back a few tears that threatened to sneak past her inner wall as she thought about her plight. *Who was she kidding? She was a dwarf. That was the gold, hard truth and nothing her mother did could change that! She might as well accept the name, no matter how hard it sounded.* But her mother still bent over backwards to protect Rosie. That made Rosie uncomfortable so she tried very hard to hide her tears. "Yes, ma'am. All ready to go."

"Let's go!" Pete, Rosie's dad, stuck his head in the front door. "We have a campground to subdue. Rosie, let me get your luggage for you. It's awfully big." He stepped in the door to grab Rosie's luggage bespangled with various soccer team logos."

Rosie tried to grab the luggage before her dad got it. She hated being coddled. "I can get it."

"It's okay if you get a little help, princess." Her dad would always think of Rosie as his little girl, even when she went away to college. *Sheesh!* Rosie thought. *Does anyone see me as anything other than a useless dwarf?* She kept that thought to herself, like she always did, and let her dad grab the bag.

The family loaded into their blue SUV, parents in the front and kids in the back seat. They left their East Memphis home to go to a campsite across the river in Arkansas. The drive took about two hours before the family reached their campsite in the fairly primitive campsite. Jimmy spent the whole trip immersed in his smartphone.

The sun was still high enough in the afternoon sky for the family to get their tents up and dinner started over a barbecue pit. They had done this enough that everyone knew what to do to get camp settled.

While they were putting the tools back in the car a medium size fuzzy brown dog ran up to Rosie. "Where did you come from?" She rubbed his soft fur. "Aren't you handsome!"

Rosie loved dogs and wished her parents would let her have one. But they said dogs were dirty and they wanted a nice, clean house. They liked things to be orderly. *I guess I kind of messed that up for them. They didn't plan on a dwarf as their oldest child.*

"Maximus, there you are." A middle aged woman with fuzzy dusty brown mid length hair, dressed in clean denim pants and a black *Celtica* t shirt came over from the next campsite and put her hand on the dog's red collar. "I told you to stay nearby, not go bothering people."

"Is this your dog? He is so friendly! I really like dogs." Rosie continued to pet Maximus.

"I'm sorry for him bothering you. He loves children, well, just about everybody." The woman smiled broadly. "I'm

Janet. Maximus and I have the campsite next door. You're welcome to come visit if your parents agree."

Rosie's face darkened and she hugged the dog. "I'll try but my parents aren't fond of dogs. I want one of my own but..." Her voice trailed off.

"Just know you're welcome. Looks like your dinner is ready so I'd better take me and Maximus back to our tent. What's your name?"

"I'm Rosie. Thank you for letting me pet Maximus." Rosie took one last swiping pet at his back as she walked away.

One more thing I can't do because I'm a dwarf, I know it. Rosie grumbled inwardly as she trundled to where her family was seated around a wooden picnic table under some very tall trees. *Mom doesn't trust me with a dog because she thinks I can't take care of one. When will they forget I'm a dwarf? Little person, hah! Makes it sound so much nicer than my life..."*
As they finished dinner and put away the washed pots, Judy, Rosie's mom, reminded Rosie and Jimmy to stay nearby. "You two remember that we are not still at home. We are in the woods with wild animals that can hurt you."

"Oh Mom..." Eight year old Jimmy whined.

Rosie just rolled her eyes and smiled, letting her mom know she heard her. "Come on, Jimmy, let's. Look around before it gets too dark." Rosie headed off towards a cleared path off of the site. Jimmy was right behind her.

The two kids headed down the stone covered path, looking under and around the ferns and bushes that lined it. The further in they walked the thicker the greenery twined around the path, covering it in spots. The thick forest around them made it difficult for Rosie and Jimmy to see the sunset. They did notice the mosquitoes that swarmed their exposed legs and arms. Both kids scratched furiously at the rising welts.

"Jimmy, it's time to head back." Rosie looked around her, suddenly aware she couldn't see the path. Even with a full moon she had trouble finding the way back to their camp.

It was too dark to see Jimmy's face as he clutched at Rosie's red t shirt sleeve. "Rosie, do you hear that?"

Both children got very quiet as they heard growling a few feet away in the darkness.

"It sounds like a dog, Rosie. Maybe he's lost."

"Maybe, Jimmy. If its Maximus, he's friendly." Rosie caught a glimpse of the path, headed for it and hauled Jimmy after her.

It was then the animal in the greenery stuck it's face out enough so Rosie could see gleaming red eyes. The growling got louder. Rosie and Jimmy sped up, hoping she was headed in the right direction. But her crooked legs just wouldn't move fast enough.

Jimmy pulled ahead of his sister. He was smaller but his straight legs could move him much faster. Rosie tried to keep up with little success. She could hear the creature drawing closer behind her. It didn't sound like Maximus.

She glanced back over her shoulder, right into the face of a large, grey wolf. It was only a few feet behind her and gaining.

Jimmy got further and further ahead as the wolf grew closer. Rosie was losing speed and tiring. Her legs were just too short.

The wolf caught her as Rosie tried to climb a small rise in the path. The wolf jumped her from behind, pinning her to the ground. Rosie passed out as the wolf rapped its teeth around her left arm.

"Rosalinda, please wake up!" Rosie's mom stood over her screaming into her face. "Baby Rosie, please wake up!"

Her dad and Jimmy were there, too, with distraught looks on their faces. Even Jimmy looked upset.

Rosie felt herself floating up from a deep sleepiness. "Mom, Dad?"

"Thank God! You're with us again." Her mom sank into the wooden chair next to Rosie's bed.

Rosie looked around her, realizing she was in a strange bed in a strange room. "Where am I?"

Rosie's dad stepped forward. "You are in a hospital room. You got bitten by a wolf in the woods. I had started looking for you when Jimmy came running in to come get you. By the time we got back to you the wolf was standing over you. It ran away when we came running at it with sticks."

"Am I okay?" Rosie only felt one wound, on her arm where she had seen the wolf bite. It had been bandaged but it ached terribly.

"You will have to have a series of rabies shots but the doctor said you are going to be fine. We were wonderfully lucky." Her father laid his right hand on her undamaged arm and glanced around the beige walled room. "You'll be going home this afternoon."

Weeks later, after the rabies shots and the stitches in her arm came out, Rosie was sitting in her room, watching some boys kick a soccer ball around the back field. It was midsummer and the moon was rising over their heads. The warm air blew through the window. Rosie noticed she could smell the late-blooming flowers and even the boys' sweaty bodies.
How strange, she thought. *I haven't been able to do that before. My sense of smell was okay but not that good. I wonder if this is part of some weird hormonal change. Am I becoming a woman now? Great! One more thing for Mom to worry about for me.*

The boys continued to play as dusk overran the field and the full moon seemed to grow brighter and larger. *Maybe she should go out and watch them play.*

Sitting in her room, Rosie felt her body begin to change, painfully. Her nose extended into a snout, her front arms lengthened and her hands pulled into paws with long claws. Her legs shortened even more, also with long claws. Meanwhile, she could feel her body becoming covered with thick, light brown fur. What was happening to her? And why are all the colors in my room so dull? She knew the many soccer posters plastering the walls and ceiling had vibrant reds and yellows, bright blues and purples. All she could see were greys and some red.

She couldn't stand up. She stood up on her all four paws (paws!) and trotted over to the full length mirror on the front of her closet door. Standing in front of her was not a little dwarf girl; it was a corgi! She had become a dog! Not even a real wolf! Rosie was a corgi!

Oh no! How could this have happened? Her parents didn't want a dog, much less their daughter to be a dog! What could she do to go back to being a girl?

About that time she felt a compulsion to go outside. Something or someone was outside. Fortunately, Rosie had left her bedroom door open or she would have been stuck inside. She trotted down the stairs, her bunny bottom plopping down each stair. She could hear her mom and dad in the TV room as she snuck by.

She made it to the front door right when her brother opened it. Rosie bee lined through the open door as Jimmy, absorbed in something on his smartphone, blindly strolled past her.

Outside, what would she do outside now? Why was she here? Who or what was she looking for? If she could have cried she would have.

The moonlight illuminated the walkway in front of her house and even the bushes' leaves reflected the light. It was a little scary but beautiful.

The bush at the side of the garage shook. Rosie watched wide eyed as a large grey wolf looked through the branches. As she watched he changed to a human woman. "Little wolf, little wolf!" A gruff voice came from the middle-aged woman. "Come over here, little wolf, before someone sees us."

She knew the woman but from where? *It was the wolf who had bitten her! What was she doing here? Should she run?* Rosie didn't know what to do.

"Do not be afraid of me. Remember me from the campsite? I'm Janet. I won't hurt you. I've never bitten a child before. I'm sorry I hurt you. Maximus and I were playing and I guess I let the wolf run wilder than usual. I'm glad you're all right. I hunted you down to help you if I could. You need to know a few things. First off, I can't change you back but I can tell you how to deal with it better."

Rosie did not know what to do. She couldn't speak and ask questions. She could run back to the house but what good would that do? Rosie needed answers and help and this looked like the only person who could help. That could be good. What could the she-wolf tell her?

So over the next hour, the older wolf told her what Rosie could do to prepare her for her new life. "When you need me, think about me and if I am any where nearby I will hear you and come back. Remember, this is a bad thing for some people but others turn it to their benefit. Look for the way to make your new wolf work for you."

When done, the she-wolf left Rosie watching the ongoing soccer game on the field. Rosie watched the soccer ball bouncing and rolling back and forth under the night lights. *Make this work for her? How? The rest of the month Rosie was a dwarf. Come the full moon she would change into a dwarf wolf, a corgi of all things!*

The soccer game was breaking up as one of the players, a brunette named Margie, walked by. "What a cute dog!" She exclaimed as she bent over to pat Rosie. "Do you live near, little cutie?"

"Is that your dog, Margie?" Another girl Rosie knew as Cindy walked up and kneeled down to reach Rosie's prick ears covered in thick light brown fur. "She's adorable. When did you get her?"

"She's not mine but I would be glad to adopt her!" Margie sat down on the grass, staining her blue and white shorts.

Cindy looked at Rosie's neck, searching for a collar and tags. "She doesn't have tags so she must be a runaway. Should we take her in to pound?"

Rosie realized this could get touchy very quickly if she got hauled to the pound. Tomorrow morning she would be back in her human form, stark naked, sitting in a cage. *Oh no! What would her parents think if they got a call like that? Would they even come get her? Of course they would but then I would have to explain that not only did they have dog in the household, it was Rosie! No, she was not ready for THAT conversation!*

While Cindy and Margie talked about what to do with this darling blonde corgi, Rosie made a run for her house. Where she had been slow as a girl, her new legs worked much better, making her as agile as any of her friends. She dodged between Cindy's thin legs, easily avoiding the coltish teen girls trying to grab her. *She might even be as fast as Mia Hamm!*

 Rosie scratched at her front door. Jimmy opened the door and she ran through his legs and to the darkened, largelu unused living room off the entry way. Evening dusk and the dark colors in the room served to make her enough shadow to hide for a few minutes. Jimmy never saw her, still absorbed in some game on his smartphone.

She waited in the shadows until she could go up the stairs to her room. Rosie stood in her dimly lit bedroom, examining her new image in the full mirror. She turned this way and that, getting as full a picture of her new body as possible.

She couldn't even be a full sized wolf! She became a dwarf wolf, which looked so much like a corgi it made no difference. The old wolf had explained it to her. Her body took the wolf template and transformed what it found. She had a dwarf body so she became a dwarf wolf. Her short arms and legs became short, dwarfish appendages. Once a month, when the moon was full Rosie would become what would look to everyone like a corgi.

Rosie was exhausted from all of the shifting and stress. She jumped up on her bed and fell asleep promptly.

The next thing Rosie knew, she awoke to sunlight sifting through the gingham curtains. "What a dream! A corgi of all things!" Then she noticed she was stark naked laying on top of a fully made bed and there were small muddy paw prints leading to it. She always slept in a cotton nightgown. Never naked! *And what about those prints? Could it have been true and not a dream?*

Rosie scrambled under the covers and lay there holding on to the chenille bedspread like it could protect her from the truth.

Rosie cringed in her familiar bed with a not so familiar thought. "I was a dog last night! OMG! What do I do next?"

Her mother answered that question by sticking her head in the doorway. "Time to get up for school, Rosie! Rise and shine!" Then she left to say the same to Jimmy.

"It seems like any other day. "Will anyone notice I'm

different?" The answer was no, no one noticed anything different about Rosie.

Her life proceeded as usual until the next full moon, when she changed again. This time, Rosie was readier. When dusk began to fall and the moon to rise, Rosie opened the door and hid behind the bed, away from the door. She had told her mother she would be at a friend's house. Rosie almost always told the truth so her mother didn't check.

When the change came, Rosie was in her room. It hurt but what could she do? She couldn't tell her parents so she endured the pain.

She was starting to feel a little better when she heard some voices outside on the soccer field. Her window was open so Rosie jumped on the bed to get a look outside. *These legs work better than my human ones. I would never be able to jump like this in my body.*

Once on the bed, Rosie could see her friends outside playing soccer. There were Cindy and Margie in their team colors. Oh, how she wanted to join them! She had wanted to play with them before but now it was a true compulsion. She had to play!

Forgetting that no one in the house knew she was a corgi, Rosie jumped off her bed, ran out of the bedroom and downstairs. Luckily, her mother had left the front door open as she unloaded groceries. Rosie slipped past her and back to the soccer field.

The soccer ball was on the ground and two girls were headed for it! But Rosie the corgi was too fast for them. She ran past one of the girls and head butted the ball towards one of the goals. Then she followed it, butting it every time one of the girls got near it.

Both sides stopped in shock.

"Who brought the dog?" One girl in a blue shirt groused. "The rules don't allow dogs!"

Cindy and Margie stopped and looked at each other. "That's the dog from last week!" Cindy was the first to say it. "Let's let her play. She's so cute! And my cousin has a corgi who plays soccer."

Margie backed her up. "Yeah, let the dog play. If we can't outplay a dog, well, maybe we need to hang up our cleats." Margie grinned from ear to ear.

"The rules say nothing about dogs. And besides, she's cute." Another girl in red grinned broadly watching Rosie move the ball around the field.

As for Rosie she paid no attention to anyone or anything except the soccer ball at the end of her nose. She was ecstatic! She was playing soccer! Granted, not the way she planned but she was actually on the field playing soccer! She was so happy she almost forgot she was a dog! She was the star on the field! Rosie couldn't have been happier as she controlled the ball, stealing it when the other side got their turn with it. She was amazing!

But nothing good lasts forever and the soccer game ended. The girls went home after petting Rosie and asking her to come play again. They didn't know she understood. Some of them even tried to get Rosie to follow them home but Rosie refused, returning to her own home when the field cleared.

Fortunately, she had eaten dinner before the game so she

slipped back in the back door and upstairs to her room. She crawled under sheets, curled up and fell fast asleep.

The next morning Rosie awoke to the sound of rain on her window but a joy she had never known in her life as a human child --she had played soccer for the first time. Maybe being a corgi once a month was okay. She may be a little person the rest of the month but for a day she could be the star, the dog who played soccer!

She lay in bed listening to the rain, a smile wrapping itself across her face as she thought about all her future soccer games. After all, she was still Rosie—just Rosie in a fur coat.

Now for that talk with her parents...\

This is story about revenge on all the puppy mill breeders. Walt Boyes is a nonfiction writer and the Editor of The Grantville Gazette, *as well as author of numerous stories set in the 1632 Universe.*

And Good With Ketchup

by Walt Boyes

It was open! The rusty wire door to the cage was open! Eric didn't know how it happened, but he pushed his small black nose at it and the door swung silently open, just enough to let him squeeze his small body through it. It was a long drop to the cracked linoleum floor, but he didn't care, because he was finally free. The only light was from the night-light over the filthy sink, but he could see well enough.

He scampered to the big steel door. Yes! There was a beat-up plastic doggie door, and it was open, so he was through it like a bullet, and raced into the exercise yard. The yard was covered with feces so deep it was hard to tell just what it was made of. Outside it was very dark, no moon. He'd never been out at night before. He wasn't used to the emotions cascading through him. Usually, he was just depressed. But now, he was exhilarated. That, and terrified! His small body shook. He ran for the bushes as a shout came from the building he'd been caged in. Eric huddled in the smallest space underneath the scraggly boxwoods that he could find, his little heart pounding and his breathing loud in his own ears. He fought to calm down.

"Goldurn best silkie terrier I ever had! And he's went missing!" Eric hid in the bushes as the sounds of cages being thrown around and animals being hurt came from the hut with all the cages.

"Aaargh! I'll catch you, you danged little rat if it's the last thing I do!" The thick steel door in the tumbledown hut slammed open, the doorway more than filled with the huge woman who had kept Eric and used him as a breeding machine. Her face was wide, with a flat nose, and she had protruding eyes and teeth, and, well, she was huge. Especially when seen from Eric's point of view. She could hold two of him in her dirty palm.

Eric knew that the bushes he was hiding in were right up against the chicken-wire fence, and that he couldn't get out that way. He waited until the huge woman was in the middle of the exercise yard and scooted through her legs, and out the gate to the road. He ran down the gravel road for a bit but she was right after him. He couldn't believe that she could move that fast! The sharp edged gravel began to punish his foot pads.

He dived off the road, his heart racing and his lungs heaving. He pushed through the deep thorny berry patch underbrush a little way off the road, and crouched, listening.

There she came, along the road, with a huge flashlight. "Come on, Eric! Come to Momma!" Her voice was treacle sweet, but there was an undertone of pure malice that Eric shook to hear. He knew if she caught him, he'd be ended. He didn't want to be ended.

Eric waited until she'd gone a little way past him, and then he burst from the bushes and plunged across the road to the open field. The blackberry thorns tore at his silkie coat and he left hanks of hair as he fled. The woman clumsily followed him through the newly ploughed dirt, as he put on as much speed as he could muster and legged it across the field. It smelled like fresh dirt, and clover, and terror, he thought.

At first, the woman was gaining on him, but Eric put on a burst of speed and got further away from her.

The moon was up now, and the field was bathed with the silver of moonlight. Eric zigged and zagged a little across the ploughed rows so he could look back and see what the woman was doing. She was still after him, and she was getting closer every minute. But in the moonlight, she looked like she had gotten bigger and her teeth had gotten longer! Eric didn't know what to make of that, but he knew it couldn't be good… so he just kept running. His heart was pounding and his breathing was beginning to sound labored. He kept running, as fast as he could.

Eric saw that the border of the field he was running toward was actually a small hill, covered in rocks. As he raced toward it, he noticed that there were some pretty big cracks in the rocks. In the moonlight they looked big enough for him to hide in.

He aimed for the biggest crack he could see. It was actually made from two big boulders that were half buried in the dirt and touching at the top. In the reflected light from the moon, they were silver gray, and he raced toward the space between them as fast as his little legs could run.

The crack wasn't very big, but he could turn around and he did. He wanted to be able to bite the woman even though he knew she would end him. He had never wanted to bite anything or anyone before, but he really wanted to bite her. Hard.

He could hear her panting as she came up to the rocks. He could see her huge black work boot right in front of the crack.

"Well, now. What have we here?" The woman chuckled in a gravelly voice. "I think I'll just lift some of these rocks out of the way!"

She grunted as she picked up the rock that made up half the crack that Eric was hiding in. He was exposed, and her big feet were blocking his way out. He stared at her, wide-eyed.

"Got ya," she laughed raucously, reaching for him with her huge hands.

Eric turned around in his length, looking for a way out. Wait! There was a deeper crack behind the other rock. He wriggled and pushed and jammed himself into the crack as her enormous hand tried to grab onto his tail. Just as her thumb and forefinger grabbed his tail tip, Eric popped through into a small, cramped space and pulled his tail free. It was dark in there, darker than anything he'd ever seen, but there was a small draft of air through the space and out the crack. It was clean, sweet-smelling air. The tiny space was shaking as the woman kicked and pounded the rocks outside, trying to force her way into the opening.

Eric caught his breath for a couple of beats, and then resolutely squeezed further into the dark hole he'd found. He popped into a bigger space, just as dark, but he had enough room that he could move. The sound of the woman trying to get into the space got softer and further away as he walked deeper into the cave, for that was apparently what he'd stumbled into. The floor of the cave was very rocky, and it hurt his already bleeding pads a little, but he kept on. The space wasn't very tall either, and in some spots he had to crawl to continue. The sound of his breathing came back to him as an echo quickly, so he knew that the space wasn't very big. But the draft of air seemed to pull him forward. There was a strange scent on the flow. It smelled like cinnamon and something else, something he didn't recognize.

He padded forward in the dark, noticing the scent was getting stronger. He followed his nose deeper into the passage, and the sound of his breathing didn't echo so much. So he knew that the space he was in was getting bigger and bigger.

He felt himself going downhill a little, and the floor was getting smoother and a little sandy. He moved forward until he bonked his nose on the wall of the cave. He realized that the passageway had turned sharply to the right, and he followed the wall. After a bit, he realized that the dark passage wasn't quite so dark any more, and he saw that it was widening out into a much bigger cave. There were huge pointy things of stone hanging from the ceiling, and sticking up from the floor of the cave. It was still really dark, and nearly everything looked gray.

The draft of air became warmer, and sort of pulsed. In and out. In and out. Eric cocked his ear, and then he used his nose to spot where it was coming from.

It was light enough in the cave to see that the draft was coming from a very large object in the corner of the cavern. He couldn't really see what it was. But he could see the three huge eggs in the center of the cavern on the sandy floor. They were mottled, and colored mostly green and brown. And they were moving.

Eric was always a curious dog, so he slowly crept closer to the eggs. First the mottled brown one started to crack, then the muddy greenish one did. The third one, which was kind of dark brownish, shook and rolled around, but no cracks appeared. Out of the first one, a sharp white egg tooth appeared in one end of the biggest crack, and it widened the crack until the egg shattered into pieces, revealing a small something. Eric didn't know what it was. It meeped at him, and he went to it and for some reason, gave it a lick. It meeped again, and huddled close to him. The next egg was also cracking, and its occupant struggled out and came toward Eric, meeping as it came. He nosed it next to the other baby whatsit, and licked it, too.

Eric noticed that the third egg, the dark brown one, was rolling violently, but not cracking. He figured that he'd better help it. So he moved toward it and bit at the end of the egg, biting into the tough leathery shell. He made enough of a hole that the egg tooth of the little thing inside the egg could come out and finish the cracking and the emergence. Eric spit out pieces of shell and lining.

Now, there were three of the whatsits, and they were all huddling with Eric and meeping at him.

Now he had time to look at them. The whatsits were all about his size, but they had leathery skin and some very fine scales, and they had big heads with large nostrils and big eyes in eye ridges. They had tails that put Eric's to shame. One was a sort of brownish beige, one was greenish, and the last one to emerge was a dull red on top with a beige belly. They crowded around Eric, and made a pile, and all three fell fast asleep. Eric was so tired from his escape that he just curled up with the whatsits and fell asleep too.

The air moving back and forth changed. Eric looked up to see a really large version of the little whatsits looking down at them, and especially looking very hard at *him*. The large whatsit was very big. Big enough that Eric had trouble seeing her head from where he was, near her feet. Her feet were silvery blue, and her claws were bigger than he was.

There was a rumble from the big whatsit. It resolved into a very deep voice. "Mmm. What do we have here? Three little dragonets and a little, what are you?" it said.

Eric decided he didn't have anything to lose, so he stood up, bristled his brownish silver fur and bottled up to twice his size, and barked fiercely at the dragon, for that was what it was, covered in red and silver scales.

"A tiny dog!" the dragon said. "And huddled in a dragonpile with my babies!" She stuck her gigantic nose in Eric's face, and without thinking, he bit her. The dragon jerked her nose away. "A fierce little dog, too!"

"Talk to me, little dog," she said, and Eric realized he could talk. He was astonished, but he said, "Please don't eat me, Mrs. Dragon!"

The dragonets were all awake by now and meeping loudly. Eric started to understand the meeping. "They think you are their brother," the dragon mother said, with a basso chuckle that made the floor rumble. "I can't eat their brother!"

"I have to go find them some food, since they aren't going to eat you," she went on. "I need to be gone for a while. Will you watch over them for me?"

Eric wasn't sure what he could do to watch them, but he nodded and yipped his assent.

"Good," said the mother dragon, "I'll be back as soon as I can. Keep them from getting too far away from the center of the cavern, dog."

"My name is Eric," he quavered bravely back.

"Good, Eric. I'll be going then." The dragon turned and slithered out of the cavern. Soon, Eric could hear the crack of unfolding wings, and her sounds decreased as she flew off to find her babies some food.

At first, everything was fine. The little dragonets slept quietly. Eric caught a nap, too. He was hugely tired, and very hungry from his escape. He nosed around the cave, finding a nice spring of water, which he lapped from, but no food.

It seemed like every time he turned around, the dragonets were getting bigger. They'd started out his size right out of the egg, but now, just a short while after the dragon herself had left him in charge, they were twice as big as he was, and getting bigger.

He decided they needed water, so he barked at them until they all got in a line, and he led them to the little spring. He drank to show them what to do, and they lined up and drank from the spring. They drank a lot, and their little stomachs bulged. They snuggled up to him, and fell asleep, there by the spring. He stared up at the stalagtites above the spring, and wondered what he was doing here. But he was free and wasn't the slave of the big woman anymore so that was good.

The little dragons weren't very good at talking. They meeped at him a lot, and he barked back, so they started imitating him. "Marf! Meep! Marf arf!" It sounded funny. He tried to teach them his name. "Eric, Eric!" he barked. "Merk, Merk, meep!" they replied.

The dragon returned, with some steaming raw, red meat. She tossed it to the three dragonets and Eric. Finally, he was able to eat something. He'd never had raw meat before, but he decided after some consideration, that he liked it. A lot. There was never a question from the dragonets, they liked the raw meat just fine. Eric wondered what it was, but he was a little afraid to ask.

Several days passed in the cavern. As the babies grew, their speech became better. Eric's did too, since he'd never practiced talking. After all, he didn't even know he could talk until he met the mother dragon.

The mother dragon named the growing dragonets. "Let's see, you're all brown, like a friar," she said to the first-born. "Your name will be Tuck." The second one she named Robin, and that left the third and lastborn. The dragon picked the reddish one up in an enormous paw and looked at her bottom. "Aha! A girl! So you'll be Marion!"

"I was always in love with the Robin Hood stories," she confided to Eric.

Eric looked puzzled. He'd never heard of Robin Hood. The lives of puppy mill dogs didn't tend much toward storytelling, or even TV. So, after everyone had had a good meal, the dragonets and Eric settled down in a big dragonpile while the mother dragon told them the story of Robin Hood and the Sherriff of Nottingham.

The mother dragon seemed to have an inexhaustible supply of stories to tell Eric and the dragonets. Every evening after their meal, she told them a new one. She told them about magical beings, too. Once she told them a story about ogres.

"That's what she is!" Eric bounced in place, barking. "That's what the woman is."

"What woman?" The mother dragon looked perturbed.

"The one I was running from when I found the cave," Eric said. "She's an ogre! She is huge, and has a flat wide face with a flat nose and big yellow cracked teeth. Two of those teeth get very long! She's a puppy miller."

"Well, I hope your ogre knows not to run afoul of dragons," the mother dragon said. "Especially since you are now an honorary dragon."

Wow, Eric thought, I'm an honorary dragon! He drew himself up to his full six-inch height, and barked, and barked! An honorary dragon! Think of that!

Several days passed. Eric taught the dragonets to play chase, and after the mother dragon brought a small ball to the cave, he taught them fetch and catch. He groomed them with his tongue, and taught them to comb his silky long hair with their raspy tongues. He taught them follow the leader, and play fighting, and all the things a responsible dog should teach puppies. The mother dragon laughed at their antics. Soon the dragonets had grown enough that Eric could ride on Tuck's or Robin's back. Marion was much smaller, and he didn't try to ride her. After the mother dragon told them a version of St. George and the dragon, Eric, Robin and Tuck played it, with Marion as the maiden prize. Eric would ride Tuck or Robin, and, since it was the dragon's version, Eric would always be roundly defeated by the lordly dragon and die bravely as the dragonet rescued the maiden.

One afternoon, as the mother dragon was out finding a nice sheep to eat, the cavern shook and shook. Huge banging noises came from the cave entrance Eric had come in originally.

His eyes wide, Eric herded the three dragonets into the back of the cave behind the spring, and after cautioning them to stay there, he crept across the cavern to the passage from which the noise was coming.

Clank-bash! The cavern shook with every blow. Something very large and heavy was banging into the rocks outside the cavern. Very cautiously, Eric crept on his belly down the passage, and finally was able to see what was going on.

There was a huge yellow machine, with a big arm and a big metal scoop on the end of it, outside the cavern. The arm kept coming down and the scoop kept banging into the rocks, making the opening of the passage bigger and bigger with every banging hit. There was a lot of dust, but Eric could see into the driver's seat of the machine. It was the ogre driving the machine, trying to break into the cavern.

The hole was getting pretty large, and Eric was getting showered with dust, dirt and rock chips. He decided to go back inside the cavern.

He found Robin, Tuck, and Marion sitting in front of the spring. They had their little dragonet wings mantled, and they were hissing. Tuck was hiccuping and finally a little pop of flame came out his mouth. Eric told them what was happening, and the little dragonets proudly told him they would defend him from the ogre.

Eric told them it would probably be better to find a way out of the cavern that little dragonets and a small silky terrier could take without being able to fly like their mother. He chivvied them back behind the spring, and took up a position in front of them to guard them.

Suddenly there was a huge crack and the whole front of the cavern fell away. There was the machine, and the ogre. The little dragons hissed and shrank back. Eric barked fiercely as the ogre came to stand in the opening.

"Well," she said. "I was looking for my dog, but I found something much better. Three lovely young dragonets. What a pretty price they'll fetch!"

She moved closer, hunkering down because she was taller and larger than the cavern. She reached a hand in, thinking to grab a dragonet. Eric raced over and bit her, twice, and danced away.

"Why you little…" the ogre cursed, whistling through her growing tusks. She was growing uglier and larger with every moment. Her arms ripped right through her sleeves, and her pants ripped down the seams as her thighs and calves tripled in size. The rest of her clothes were ripping as she grew.

Eric continued to run forward, bite, and run away. He kept it up even though the ogre was grabbing for him with one hand and trying to pound him flat with the other. He got hold of her ankle, and bit, hanging on. She shook her leg, sending him flying into the wall. He hit hard. He lay there for a moment, then leaped up, shook himself, and dashed back and bit her again.

Robin mantled. "You hurt our brother," he squeeked. "Blurp!" Tuck made a little fire appear on his nose. Even Marion tried to snarl at the ogre.

"Now, now, little dragons," the ogre tried to coo. "You'll love it living with me, just like Eric did, and will again!" She tried to pound Eric again, and he again was just able to get away.

"I don't think they'll love living with you," a deep and angry voice said from the dark in the back of the cave.

Mother dragon emerged, her reddish scales shining like they had fire within them. She was much bigger than the ogre, and the ogre shrank back a little.

"I…I…" The ogre began, holding her big hands out as if to explain.

The mother dragon looked at Eric. "Take the children out back in the cavern, Eric. They shouldn't see this."

Eric herded Tuck, Robin, and Marion into the back of the cavern. As they went into another smaller cave, he heard behind him a banging.

"Never!"

Bang!

"Mess!"

Bang!

"About!"

Bang!

"With!"

Bang Bang Bang!

"Dragons!"

Bang!

"Because," the dragon said, muffled by a full mouth, "Thou art crispy, and good with ketchup!"

Jean Rabe is a New York Times bestselling author who has, among her numerous credits, worked with the likes of Andre Norton and has novels and short stories in many genres. Neither first appeared in Imaginary Friends *(Daw Books). You may never look at a stray dog the same way again after reading this story.*

Neither

By Jean Rabe

The age-faded sign read: "Please don't give money to the vagrants. They are either professional beggars or addicts who use the money for drugs or booze."

Sig was neither.

He was a beggar, but certainly not a professional. A professional would be good at it and would have enough coins in his outstretched paper cup to buy something decent to eat. And he wasn't an addict, at least not anymore. Sig used to drink more than a little bit of whatever was strong and cheap or could be found in near-empty bottles discarded behind the Wild Horse Saloon. He'd been sober for the better part of two years.

When he drank, his senses got so muddled he couldn't properly hear the music, and he could barely see the dog.

It was a good dog.

Sig sat on a clean piece of sidewalk along Broadway in downtown Nashville. His back against the red brick of the T-shirt shop, his head came up just far enough to obscure the lower corner of the front window that displayed the vagrancy sign. There were plenty of vagrancy notices in downtown Nashville, but most of the beggars avoided sitting directly beneath them. Sig sat here for several hours every day because the dog favored this spot. It was a convenient location from which to hear the music drifting out of the various bars.

The dog obviously didn't mind the fare that roiled off the juke boxes in the diners, but it seemed to like the live music the best, feeling the beat from trap sets and basses pulsing through the concrete and reverberating against its paws. Sig could feel the beat, too, when he set his fingertips against the sidewalk and concentrated, as he was doing now. It was the heartbeat of the city, and it brought out the people—the regulars who lived and worked in the area, the bums like himself who preferred the freedom and sounds of the colorful sidewalks to the blandness of the homeless shelters, and most importantly it brought out the tourists, who occasionally tossed scraps to the dog.

The city was said to have a black heart, and that the beat masked it with lively tunes and sad songs, with electric guitars and expensive mandolins, with busty girls lip-sinking for videos that would be played on CMT—all of it distracting folks so they didn't look too closely. But Sig looked. And the city's dark heart showed itself to him from time to time on this very sidewalk in the forms of pickpockets and purse snatchers—several of which the dog had thwarted through the years at Sig's encouragement. Sig had also spotted drugs and money changing hands on a few corners after sunset; the dog had fouled a few of those sales, too.

A very good dog.

Sig liked bluegrass the best, even when the singers wailed too loudly in off-key feigned country voices, as someone was doing this very minute. The dog's preference? It didn't seem to matter: western swing, rockabilly, traditional, folk, honky-tonk, gospel, country-rock, swamp opera, or boogie-woogie. Sig figured the dog liked just about everything— except for that damned accordion that started wheezing almost every afternoon from an apartment just above Ernest Tubb's Record Shop across the street. The dog howled like a coon hound when the accordion played.

The dog came to just above Sig's knees, the shade of an expensive Gibson mahogany guitar, with large, kind eyes and sharply pointed ears that were always tipped toward whatever joint was offering the best music at any given time. It looked like one of the street artists had lovingly dry brushed white paint against the dog's otherwise dark muzzle and just above its eyes to give it brows. Just a hint of age to the dog. Distinguished looking.

Sig could not have imagined a more wonderful, beautiful dog.

He didn't know how old the dog was, only that he'd spotted it in an ally some six or seven years ago, or maybe it was eight, sniffing around a trash bin it couldn't quite reach. Sig had rummaged in the bin for it that night, coming up with some soggy French fries and a few partially eaten pork chops, which they shared. They'd been together ever since that night—except for when Sig had been drinking.

They slept in the morning when the music was dead, in the hazy time between three and nine when they would find a Dumpster in an alley to curl up behind so the light from the bare bulbs that hung above back doors didn't quite reach them. The air was always dead then, too, and was thick with sweat and filth and rotting lettuce and cabbage and whatever else had spoiled in restaurant kitchens and had subsequently been tossed out.

Promptly at nine, when the music started up again, they'd rise as if to an alarm clock. They'd stroll out to the sidewalk and sit in their spot. They'd wait for breakfast, which if Lee didn't stop by would consist of donut halves tossed in the trash can on the corner—of which they had a perfect view—or sometimes there'd be remnants of those sausage and egg sandwiches that the tourists bought at fast food shops and found too greasy to finish. Grease rarely bothered Sig and the dog.

It was such a good, good dog.

"Lee's late," Sig mused. She was special to him. She was one of the few people on Broadway who never looked the other way when she passed Sig and the dog. A bartender at Legends on the Corner, she always stopped on her way to work each morning. Sometimes she gave them leftovers after her shift was over. Lee worked from nine to five, and so her comings and goings fit rather well with traditional mealtimes.

Sig always looked forward to seeing her. Lee's skin was the color of pale peaches, even-toned except for a hint of blush on her cheeks. And her hair was long and dark and always gleaming, her teeth as white and sparkling as new snow. Sig's own hair was always a tangled buggy mess, and so he kept it stuffed up under an old Tennessee Titans cap so not to offend people.

Her smile . . . well it was beyond Sig's ability to describe. It melted him, made it difficult for him to think and to breathe, and it always set the dog's tail to wagging goofily.

She wouldn't always be a bartender, Sig knew. He'd heard her sing. Sometimes they'd shuffle down to Legends, and go around the corner to the side door, which was always open. They'd sit and listen to the young men playing acoustic guitars and hawking their CDs between sets. Every once in a while, on afternoons when business was slow, Lee would come out from behind the bar and sing a couple of songs she'd written.

"You're gonna be a star," Sig told her once. It was just a matter of time until she was discovered and swept away from this life. "You're gonna be at the Opry someday, Lee. Name in flashing lights."

"Me and everyone else on Broadway'll be there," she'd return with a dazzling snowy smile.

"She should've been here by now," Sig told the dog. "Not like Lee to be late." He craned his neck this way and that, thinking maybe she had to park somewhere else this morning and had went in Legend's side door and thereby missed them. "Maybe she's sick. Not like her to be sick, though." He couldn't remember a time when Lee had been anything but perfect. "Not like her at all."

The dog tipped its ears toward Tootsie's, just a few doors down, where a man who sounded vaguely like Kris Kristoferson had begun a set. The dog pressed its front paws against the sidewalk and Sig set his paper cup down and did the same with the palms of his hands, both of them feeling the steady beat rise through the concrete.

Shortly after the accordion started that afternoon, Sig rose and gestured for the dog to follow; its howling was bothering the T-shirt shop customers. They ambled up the street, past Tootsies, where Sig paused to peer inside. Sig didn't care much for the place, and was glad Lee hadn't been hired there. "World Famous" maybe, but it looked more ragged than his scruffy self. It was murky inside, always, the shadows helping to mask the cobwebs in the corners and the spilt beer on the floor. And it had a fusty pong that made even his nose wrinkle. The walls were interesting, though. They were papered with autographed photos of country music stars, all of them curled on the edges and yellowed from decades of cigarette smoke.

A bartender frowned and waived a towel at a horsefly. But Sig knew the gesture was aimed at him.

"Just looking," Sig said. He ducked back out and continued west, the dog dutifully following. He stopped at a plastic Elvis, little bigger than life-sized, arms outstretched waiting for a tourist to step into his embrace for a photograph. The dog hiked its leg and peed on the king's pantleg.

"Ain't you got no respect?" Sig asked the dog. But he smirked and winked. The dog always peed on the king.

They went around the corner and headed to Legend's side door. Sig looked in, sniffed, and scratched at his ear. At his feet, the dog did the same. Elvis's first five records were framed on one wall. Sig had heard they were worth thousands, the only five recorded on 78 RPMs on Sun Records. Kabuki-faced Kiss dolls were on a shelf near a large portrait of Johnny Cash and a guitar gaudily covered with shells and buttons. A saxophone, trombone, and a sitar hung near the ceiling. Album covers, some of them signed, were everywhere.

A guy with a battered guitar was singing about the 'hits of the day' at a place called the Roadkill Café. Cute music, Sig thought, scowling. "Get to the serious stuff."

When Sig stood at the side door sometimes Lee would come out and bring him a soda or coffee, and the dog a cup of water. Sometimes a sack of microwave popcorn, still warm. But he couldn't see her inside, not behind the bar or at any of the tables, and not around the stage with the roadkill man. Maybe she was in the kitchen or in the bathroom. Maybe she was getting ready to sing a song or two, as the customers were few and didn't look to be demanding much attention. Sig tuned out the roadkill man and kept glancing around.

Sheet music and photographs were displayed here and there, none of them yellowed like at Tootsie's. A notice, but not for vagrancy. It offered a reward of $100 for anyone reporting pilfering of the memorabilia. A sequined shirt that would have been worthy of Porter Wagoner caught his eye. Framed dollar bills, Canadian and US, hung behind the bar. There were lots of things to ogle in this place.

"That'd be nice, wouldn't it?" Sig mused, eyeing the reward notice again. "Get me a night in a hotel, a hot bath, get you a flea dip. A soft bed for us to sleep on for once. Get me a new shirt, too. Maybe like that sequined one. A pretty collar for you."

The dog's nose was pointed down the street, quivering in the direction of the Ryman Auditorium. A gang of toughs in the back parking lot were admiring each other's tattoos.

"Maybe Lee's got a new job, dog. Maybe she went back to school."

She'd told them once that she was going to be a veterinarian . . . once upon a time . . . before she decided to move to Nashville and look for her big break, singing and songwriting. Sig remembered her saying that one of her songs was being considered by Tanya Tucker or Loretta Lynn or somebody else famous.

"Maybe some big record producer discovered her, dog. She would've told us, though, don't you think?"

The dog growled softly, and the hair rose in a ridge along its back. The toughs were parting ways, but two of them lagged behind, eyes fixed on the steps leading to the Ryman's backdoor.

Sig returned his attention to the barroom. "Dog, maybe I should call you Shep." He'd spotted a piece of sheet music called "Old Shep," by Red Foley, autographed and displayed behind a square of plastic in the hallway that led to Legends' bathrooms. "Elvis sang that." He looked down at the dog. "That leg you like to pee on? That's Elvis. He recorded 'Old Shep' some time ago. Sad, sad song. Not really country, though Elvis gave it a little twang. Do you want a name, dog?"

The dog continued to rumble at the two toughs until they eventually left; their eyes on the pavement as they passed by Sig, voices low in a conspiratorial whisper.

Sig settled down just outside the door, back against the brick, legs stretched out. The roadkill man started singing about cigars and former presidents. "Get to the serious stuff," Sig repeated.

The dog nestled next to him, paws firmly against the sidewalk to better feel the beat, chin on Sig's knee.

"You're a good, good dog," Sig said.

They dozed until just before sunset, when a tour bus pulled up belching smoke and offloading a bevy of blue-haired women and balding men, the driver ushering them in the side door, all of them doing their best to ignore Sig and the dog. Not one dropped a coin in his paper cup. He listened to them shuffling across the hardwood floor, imagined them gaping at the memorabilia on the wall, prayed that one of them would take something—maybe one of those ugly Kiss dolls so the dog would thwart them and gain Sig a reward.

"That hundred bucks would buy us a fancy time," Sig told the dog.

The dog listened to the people, too, but also to the music. The roadkill man had packed up his guitar some time ago, replaced now by a five-piece group with a well-known bluegrass man on keyboards. They'd been playing something soft until the tourists came in. Cranking up the volume now, a little thing with a big high-pitched voice started singing country-pop. Sig thought she was pretty good, her five-piece band that barely fit on the stage a bit better.

Not as good as Lee, though. Not close.

Two songs later the tourists shuffled back out, and a few of them dropped pieces of pizza crust on the sidewalk for the dog.

Shortly after sunset the rain started, making the street look like a slick black snake that wound its way past Legends and the back of the Ryman. The streetlights flickered on, and the neon beer signs sparked bright, sending rivulets of color streaming down the windows and across the sidewalk. The music got louder, still the little thing singing, sounding like Cyndi Lauper with a country twist. Hard to pick out all the words to her song, as a large crowd had gathered inside, and the quiet conversations, punctuated by calls for the bartender, mingled with the lyrics.

Sig knew there'd be a crowd at Tootsie's, too, and at all the other spots around the corner on Broadway. Music City's pulse quickened after dark, regardless of the weather. The beat brought more and more folks out the later the hour got.

Sig lolled his head back and closed his eyes, faintly heard the rain pattering on the sidewalk and felt its feeble attempt to clean the grime off his face. Soon he imagined that he'd be getting a good whiff of the dog. It always picked up a musty funk when it got wet. Sig certainly could pick out all the good things cooking inside: potato skins and roast beef sandwiches, mini-pizzas and popcorn. Sig had an amazing sense of smell.

"I'm hungry," Sig told the dog.

Glasses clinked and a cheer went up. It was somebody's birthday.

"You don't mind the rain, the two of you?"

Sig's eyes flew open.

Lee stood in front of him with a hand on one hip, an umbrella held in the other. Black pants and white shirt, face shadowed except for her incredible smile.

"I'm on the late shift for a few days, filling in for Karen," she explained.

Sig smiled back. He was always at a loss for words in her presence. Maybe she thought him mute. The dog wagged its tail goofily and gave her a soft bark.

"I'll bring you out something on my break. Do you like roast beef?"

Sig nodded.

"Coffee?"

Another nod.

She looked at her watch and stepped into the doorway, taking down her umbrella and shaking it off before she disappeared into the crowd. Sig imagined he heard her high heels clicking against the hardwood.

He knew she wouldn't be singing tonight. Too many customers, all of them too demanding on the bartenders. He suspected that's why she liked the day shift, not as many people, meaning she had more opportunities to sing. He rested his head back against the wall, ignored the rain, and waited.

Sig didn't notice the dog pad away, down to the corner so it could raise its leg on the king again. And he didn't notice the beat of the city alter beneath his fingertips, heralding the reemergence of the two tattooed toughs that had walked by before. If Sig had been watching, he would have noticed that they'd changed clothes, or rather had added to what they'd been wearing earlier. Each had a black longcoat, a little too big with the shoulder seams drooping halfway down their arms. The toughs went in Legends' side door.

If Sig had been alert, he might have heard the first shout of surprise coming from the barroom, cutting above the music as the two men wrenched the big frame off the wall holding Elvis's five 78s. Instead, Sig was rudely jostled awake by the dog, returned from its pee break and now yapping.

"What?" Sig reached out to scratch the dog's ears, but then realized something was amiss inside. He got up, nearly slipping on the slick sidewalk, steadying himself against the wall as the two men forced their way out, the bulky frame held beneath the larger man's longcoat. They started to run.

Sig tried to take it all in, but everything came at him so quickly. The dog was still barking, people shouted, a whistle blew.

"Call the police!" someone inside hollered.

Suddenly Lee was out the door, a gun in her hand. She sidestepped Sig and dashed down the sidewalk, following the two men who were fast losing themselves in the shadows that stretched out from the back of the old Ryman Auditorium. The dog barked a staccato rhythm that jolted Sig into action.

"A robbery," Sig stated. "Lee's after them." Then he and the dog gave chase.

Others came in their wake, but not as fast. They were curious patrons, mostly, wanting to see if the men were going to be caught and not wanting to get too wet. None of them ventured past the Ryman. The rain was coming harder now, rat-a-tat-tatting against the pavement and against the two thieves' longcoats, against Sig and Lee and the dog's back.

Car horns bleated from somewhere behind them on Broadway, and music poured out of the honky-tonks and dinner theaters and from open windows of apartments. The beat pulsed up through the sidewalk and into Sig's feet, and he set his legs to pump in time with it, his old shoes slap, slap, slapping against the wet sidewalk, the rain rat-a-tat-tatting, the music blaring, the beat coming louder and harder and not doing a good job right now to mask the city's black heart.

"He's got the Elvis records!" someone shouted from well behind them.

"The seventy-eights!" another called.

The dog was just ahead of Sig, loping along at what looked like an easy pace, closing the distance to Lee, and then passing her.

A very, very good dog.

Their course took them farther from the downtown, the lights getting dimmer here, the music softer, the rain coming louder, and thunder booming and rattling windows. A siren keened.

"Get 'em, dog," Sig urged.

The thunder rattled the windows of an old apartment building they ran by.

Sig balled his hands into fists, swung his arms, and gulped in the wet air. He lost his Titans cap and felt his hair fly free, whipping the back of his neck.

A taxi cruised by, slowed, and the driver rolled down the window. He shouted something that Sig couldn't hear, was shouting at the dog and the two men, then rolling up his window and driving away.

Around another corner the thieves dashed, this street better lit.

Lee dropped to a knee and fired. She was a good shot, and the bullet slammed into the concrete near the larger man's feet. The dog growled and the men stopped and spun. The smaller one pulled out his own gun.

The beat of the city changed again, pulsing now in a syncopated rhythm that felt uncomfortable against Sig's feet. He felt his heart rising into his throat, his chest grow tight. He tried to call out to the dog, which was heading straight toward the man with the gun.

Don't let it be like the song, Sig prayed. He remembered Elvis 's recording of 'Old Shep,' the king singing about having to shoot the dog because it was old and the vet couldn't do anything for it.

The dog was pretty much everything to Sig.

Another shot rang out and Sig closed his eyes. He didn't see the pavement chip up at the dog's feet. He didn't see the dog vault off the sidewalk, pads losing contact with the pulsing beat of the city and ramming into the chest of the tough with the gun. He didn't see the dog tear at Nashville's black heart when it sunk its teeth into the tough's cheek.

But Sig heard the man scream and heard the clatter of a gun striking the pavement, and he heard the baying sound the dog made just like when the accordion started up. He heard the clack-clack-clack of Lee's high heels and, finally, he heard a siren come louder.

Sig opened his eyes.

The larger man stood riveted, watching the dog maul his companion. He cursed when the police car pulled up, the red and blue lights playing against an old apartment building. The framed 78s slipped from beneath the thief's coat and landed to lean against his leg.

The dog took another bite out of the downed man, who moaned softly.

"Put your hands up!" A car door squeaked open as a burly policeman got out. "Do it now!"

The larger man complied, eyes still on the dog.

"Should I shoot the mongrel?" This came from the other cop.

"No," Sig croaked. "Please no."

"No," the first policeman answered. "It's just a stray. Seen it hanging around on Broadway a few times. I'd say it did us a favor."

The dog backed off and shook its head, blood flying from its muzzle. It trotted toward Sig and Lee, all of them standing in the driving rain.

"Good dog," one of the cops said. "Good, good dog."

The dog wagged its tail and retreated the way it had come, Lee following, heading back to Broadway. Sig waited a moment, watching the cops load the two men and the framed 78s into the car, listening as one of them got on the radio and reported their success.

"A hundred dollars," Sig said. "If we get that reward, I'll buy us something fancy." It took him a few minutes to catch up to Lee and the dog and to set his feet in time to the beat of the city again.

The dog continued to wag its tail, happy over the excitement of the past several minutes. Good thing Lee's 'work schedule' had changed, the dog thought, otherwise this very real robbery might have been missed.

Sig should get a reward for his part in this, the dog decided, even though no real money would come the bum's way. Sig could 'buy' a new shirt and a new pair of pants, a new Tennessee Titans ball cap and get a proper haircut, maybe even think he'd passed the night in a hotel. And the dog would reward Lee, too, let her think she was getting her big break and that Tanya Tucker and Loretta Lynn were vying to record her song.

Lee and Sig were the best imaginary friends a good dog could have.

Neither of them real. Except in the dog's mind.

I was watching our Corgi Toby go about his rounds and it occurred to me that it looked like he was preparing to save the world. Then the next thing I know this story showed up in the Heroes Best Friend *anthology by Seventh Star Press.*

Toby and Steve Save the World

by Joy Ward

Toby officiously tripped down the wooden-floored hallway, his almost tailless bunny butt proudly swinging from side-to-side. Yes! He had saved the day once again! The red and white Pembroke Corgi grinned to himself. If he could have reached his little white left front foot around he would have been patting himself on his back. Toby couldn't do that so he pranced down the hall. He felt like the biggest. baddest Corgi in the world (or at least in North America)!

And so he should. Toby had just saved the world one more time. Okay, Toby hadn't actually been the one doing the saving but he had made sure his human, Steve, had done it. Steve with his voice, human form and opposable thumbs carried through the actions but Toby knew that Toby was the one in charge when Steve did his best. Steve was well known for being in the right place when someone was in danger and showing up at the right time to oh, catch the baby falling out of a tenth story window, block the entrance of an armed schizophrenic from entering a grade school or even intercept a confirmed sex offender from climbing in a ten-year-old girl's bedroom window.

Yes, Steve had been the human doing those things but nobody knew that without Toby Steve would never have shown up at the right time for any of those deeds. Toby was the one responsible for getting Steve to the right spot at the right time. Without Toby, Steve was just a really big, strong human male with good intentions.

As Toby sat congratulating himself on their most recent success over evil, he felt that pricking in his huge triangular ears that meant it was time to jump into action again. He sat quietly for the merest moment as he listened to find the potential bad guy or girl. At first all he could here was the large, brownish dog down the alley barking at two obnoxious male human teens as they strolled down the alley. One of them was making a pain of himself by slapping a stick across the fences along the alley. Were these the humans about to cause serious trouble? The question went out to Toby's friend, Blaze, the dog who was barking. "No," Blaze sent back. "These old pups walk this was every day, doing the same useless tricks. No real danger here."

Toby turned his fuzzy head this way and that, looking for the danger to address.

All of a sudden, Toby caught the mental scent. Sweetie, a two-year-old Pomeranian a few streets over, was frantically sending a call for help. The young bitch was jumping up and down calling for Toby's help and attention.

"Defender! Defender! Help! Help! Bring your human! Need you next door!"

"This is Toby. What is the need? How can we help?" Toby sent his thoughts back to the obviously panicked young girl.

"Fire! Fire! Fire next door. No adult humans nearby. Two human pups in back room. They are sleeping and don't know. Help soon!"

Toby leaped up, making sure he knew exactly where the Pomeranian lived. It was mid-afternoon so Steve was in his office typing on his metal box. It could be hard to get Steve moving in that case but Toby was the area Defender, charged with keeping his area safe by working with his human. Okay, time to make Steve think Toby HAD to go walkies.

Toby prepared himself for a performance as he zoomed into Steve's office. Sure enough, Steve sat in his big, rolling chair moving his fingers across the metal case on his desk. The speed of the taps told Toby that Steve was deeply into this piece. Toby would just have to pull out all his tricks to get Steve moving!

Toby started with his opening gambit by placing himself directly behind Steve's chair. He braced himself and let out a series of piercing barks. "Bark! Bark!" He stopped a second and then started barking again. "Bark! Bark! Bark!"

Steve almost fell off his chair as the barks hit with full force on the immense, twenty-seven-year-old man with curly brown hair tumbling to his shoulders. "Whoa, Toby! What the hell is your problem? We just got in a few hours ago. Surely, you don't have to pee again this soon. Shut up!"

Toby backed up a foot or so to let Steve know that he really did have to go walkies.

"Can't you wait? You're not an old dog and I'm really into this article now. It's going right where I want it to go."

Yeah, but I have somewhere else for you to go RIGHT NOW! Toby thought as hard as he could at Steve with another increasingly sharp bark to punctuate the thoughts. "Now, now, now!" Like a drummer pounding out notes, Toby pushed each "now" with stronger and stronger barks.

Steve looked disgusted as he hit a key on his metal box and pushed his chair back from the desk. "Dang, Toby. You just have no respect for my time, do you?"

Toby redoubled his efforts to get Steve moving by jumping up as he barked. Steve was moving now but not fast enough. Toby had to get him moving faster. Okay, let's put this into high gear, he told himself.

Toby started gagging. It wasn't hard since he could throw up at will. A bit of bad grass here or decayed bird there and there sat a little pile of stomach contents. "Ack!" Toby let the sound and the sight of potential vomit fill the room. Just to make sure Steve got the message Toby hit it again, hard. "Ack, ack, ack!"

Now Steve started moving! "Hold that, Toby! I'm moving! I'm moving!" Toby knew Steve hated cleaning vomit off the beautiful wooden floors. He would do almost anything to keep Toby from throwing up on his beloved floors. Toby didn't understand it but he did know how to use that fear to motivate Steve. And right now Toby needed Steve to get really motivated, and fast!

Steve shoved his huge feet into the boots sitting next to the desk, grabbed his denim jacket and pulled Toby's blue leash out of the closet behind him. "Let's go, pukey!"

Toby hated to be teased but he would do what he had to save the little humans. He was the Defender! Let Steve call him pukey or even stinky like he did when Toby had eaten too much dog food if Toby could do his job.

As Toby was getting Steve out of the apartment and down the front steps he could hear Sweetie's frantic barks. "Help, Toby! Fire faster, bigger! Come! Come! Now! Now!" He could sense her jumping up like a cotton ball blown by a mad wind as she bounced against her glass front door. Toby had to get Steve moving faster!

There! Toby could smell just a whiff of the fire. But he knew Steve's puny nose would not help him recognize the danger. Toby had to get Steve within a human's smelling range.

Steve and Toby got down the front steps when Toby hit the end of his leash hard. "Come on, Steve! Come on, Steve! Move! Move! Move!" Once again, Toby was frustrated by how deaf humans were, including his mostly wonderful Steve. Somehow Steve could only hear wordless barks instead of the messages Toby tried so hard to mentally push to him. How could humans be so deaf?

"Toby, not so fast. You'll pull me down. Just pick a spot to urp and do it! One place is as good as another. Come on!"

Toby mentally shook his head and continued massive pulls on the leash, oh so slowly hauling his reluctant hero behind him.

Foot by foot Toby leaned against the leash as he moved Steve closer and closer to the endangered children. "Please let us be on time," Toby prayed to Sirius, the dog god. All Toby could hear was the blood pounding in his head and Sweetie's frenzied barks.

Finally, Steve realized he was needed a block ahead. "Do you smell that, Toby? I think I smell fire up ahead. Let's speed up!" Now the tables turned and Steve led the way as he pulled on Toby's leash. Steve was almost dragging Toby down the dry sidewalk.

Then Toby could hear Sweetie. "Sweetie, we're here. We're here."

Sweetie's barks got faster. "Yay! Yay! Children still in house and asleep! Humans lock front door but not back. Go to back door, Defender!"

Steve was running faster now. Toby was having trouble keeping up with the human. Toby's short dwarfed legs were not meant to move this fast but he did. They flashed like white rabbit paws right behind Steve's long strides. An onlooker might only have seen the flash of red and white at Steve's denim-covered legs as they raced, man and Defender at his heels.

Toby knew which house so he had to get in front. He put on a burst of speed, throwing himself at Steve's feet to make him stop in front of the right house. Toby could smell the fire and he had Sweetie's help but Steve could wander around until the flames emerged and the children were dead. Toby had to move Steve to the right house immediately.

"Toby, what the hell are you doing? You almost tripped me up." Steve yelled at Toby but Toby had stopped him in front of the right house.

Steve turned around, sniffing the air. How did they use those tiny noses? The thought flashed across Toby's mind. No time for that thought. Toby had Steve at the right house but he still had to get Steve in the house.

Steve ran to the front door, simultaneously pumping the door bell and pounding on the metal door. No way to get in here. Toby had to pull Steve to the back.

Toby pulled violently towards the side of the house. Steve looked at Toby then back to the invincible metal door in front of him. "Let's see if there's another way in." The leash suddenly went slack as Steve followed Toby around the house to the back door.

By now, the smoke was starting to leak under the slightly raised windows next to the back door. Steve wasted no time knocking on the stained metal door. "If this door is locked, Toby, I'm not sure what we can do." He grabbed the handle and yanked the door open. Smoke almost knocked him over.

Toby could hear the two humans screaming one room over. Steve obviously could hear them but not tell where they were. He was coughing up smoke as he tried to see through the smoke. Toby grabbed his leash in his mouth, forcibly leading Steve to the children. Steve dropped Toby's leash and swept up a child in each arm. Within a moment or two Steve, the children and Defender Toby were out of the house ad on the grass across the street. The humans fell on the ground coughing up black saliva. Everyone was safe thanks to Steve and Toby, though only Steve would get the credit they both deserved.

Sweetie was right! Would anyone know she shared this victory? Probably not. Humans tended to look around for human heroes. She had called the Defender and his human. So often the Defenders and their fellow dogs were the real heroes but humans, head blind as usual, didn't see that. Oh well.

Later as Toby laid on his doggie bed in the family room, munching on one of his favorite crunchy treats, Toby thought about how funny humans were. Steve is a good man but even he doesn't suspect he has help being in the right place at the right time. But what the heck? Toby loved defending his neighborhood, his world. He didn't need the humans' appreciation. He could hear Sweetie's contented barks as she slept on her human's couch. She dreamed of her part in the day, her tiny legs moving in the air above her. He could also sense Blaze's nightly intention to make his daily stand against the two obnoxious boys, along with all the thoughts and wishes and loves of the other canine in his area. He didn't care that the humans didn't know he was the Defender and Steve got all the credit. Toby had Steve, a warm home and these oh so tasty treats. Who needs fame when he could sleep on The Bed with Steve and help Steve defend their area? Toby loved his life! Life was good!

Toby crunched his treat and waited for the next call to save the world.

It is impossible to have anything to do with science fiction, and fantasy without being familiar with Mike Resnick, if for no other reason than he has won more awards in science fiction that anyone—ever. He is currently the Editor of Galaxy's Edge Magazine. Blue won the American Dog Writers Award for Best Short Fiction in 1978. It first appeared in American Hunting Dog Magazine.

BLUE

by Mike Resnick

I had a dog, his name was Blue.
Bet you five dollars he's a good one too.
Come on, Blue!
I'm a-coming too.

They sing that song about him, Burl Ives and Win Stracke and the rest, but they wouldn't have been too happy to be locked in the same room with old Blue. He'd as soon take your hand off as look at you.

He wandered out to my shack one day when he was a pup and just plumped himself down and stayed. I always figured he stuck around because I was the only thing he'd ever seen that was even meaner and uglier than he was.

As for betting five dollars on Blue or anything else, forget it. It's been so long since I've seen five dollars that I don't even remember whose picture is on the bill. Jefferson, I think, or maybe Roosevelt. Money just never mattered much to me, and as long as Blue was warm and dry and had a full belly, nothing much mattered to him.

Each winter we'd shaggy up, me on my face and him just about everywhere, and each summer we'd naked down. Didn't see a lot of people any time of year. When we did, it'd be a contest to see who could run them off the territory first, me or Blue. He'd win more often than not. He never came back looking for praise, or like he'd done a bright thing; it was more like he'd done a *necessary* thing. Those woods and that river was ours, his and mine, and we didn't see any reason to put up with a batch of intruders, neither city-slickers nor down-home boys either.

It was a pretty good life. Neither of us got fat, but we didn't go hungry very often either. And it was kind of good to sit by a fire together, me smoking and him snorting. I don't think he liked my pipe tobacco, but we had this kind of pact not to bother each other, and he stuck by it a lot better than a couple of women I outlived.

And, Mister, that dog was hell on a cold scent.

Blue chased a possum up a cinnamon
 tree.
Blue looked at the possum, possum
 looked at me.
Come on, Blue.
I'm a-coming, too.

Except that it wasn't a cinnamon tree at all. I don't ever recollect seeing one. It was just a plain old tree, and I still can't figure out how the possum got up there all in one piece.

It must have been twenty below zero, and neither of us had eaten in a couple of days. Suddenly Blue put his nose to the ground and started baying just like a bloodhound. Thought he was on the trail of an escaped killer the way he carried on, but it was just an old possum, looking every bit as cold and hungry as we did. The way Blue ran him I thought his heart would burst, but somehow he made it a few feet up the tree trunk. Slashed Blue on the nose a couple of times, just for good measure, but if he thought that would make old Blue run off with his tail between his legs, he had another think coming. Blue just stood there, kind of smiling up at him, and saying, Possum, let's see you come on down and try that again.

It was a mighty toothy smile.

Baked that possum good and brown.
Laid sweet potatoes all around.
Come on, Blue,
You can have some too.

Never did like possum meat. Even when you bake a possum it tastes just awful. The sweet potatoes were just to kill the flavor. Folksingers and poets live on steak and praise; let 'em try living on possum for a few days and I bet that verse would come out different.

Anyway, I did offer some to Blue, just like the song says. He looked at it, picked it up, and kind of played with it like a pup dog does when you give him a piece of fruit. At first I thought it was just good taste on Blue's part, but then his nose started to swell where the possum had nailed him. Usually I'd slap a little mud on a wound like that, but mud's not the easiest thing to come by when it's below zero, so I rubbed some snow on instead.

First time in his life Blue ever snarled at me.

When old Blue died he died so hard,
He jarred the ground in my back yard.
Go on, Blue.
I'll get there too.

Guess the possum had rabies or something, because Blue just got worse and worse. His face swelled up like a balloon, and some of the fire went out of his eyes.

We stayed in the shack, me tending to him except when I had to go out and shoot us something to eat, and him just getting thinner and thinner. I kept trying to make him rest easier, and I could see him fighting with himself, trying not to bite me when I touched him where it hurt.

Then one day he started foaming at the mouth, and howling something awful. And suddenly he turned toward me and got up on his feet, kind of shaky-like, and I could tell he didn't know who I was any more. He went for me, but fell over on his side before he got halfway across the floor.

I only had a handful of bullets left to last out the winter, but I figured I'd rather eat fish for a month than let him lie there like that. I walked over to him and put my finger on the trigger, and suddenly he stopped tossing around and held stock-still. Maybe he knew what I was going to do, or more likely it was just that he always held still when I raised my rifle. I don't know the reason, but I know we each made things a little easier for the other in that last couple of seconds before I squeezed the trigger.

When I get to Heaven, first thing I'll do
Is grab my horn and call for Blue.
Hello, Blue.
Finally got here too.

That's the way the song ends. It's a right pretty sentiment,
so I suppose they had to sing it that way, but Heaven ain't
where I'm bound. Wouldn't like it anyhow; white robes and
harp-strumming and minding my manners every second.
Besides, winter has always chilled me to the bone; I *like*
heat.

But when I get to where I'm going, I'll look up and call for
him, and Blue will come running just like he always did.
He'll have a long way to go before he finds me, but that
never stopped old Blue. He'll just put his nose to the
ground, and pretty soon we'll be together again, and he'll
know why I did what I did to him.

And we'll sit down before the biggest fire of all, me
smoking my pipe and him twitching and snorting like
always. And maybe I'll pet him, but probably I won't, and
maybe he'll lick me, but probably he won't. We'll just sit
there together, and we'll know everything's okay again.

Hello, Blue. I finally got here too.

Have you ever wondered where a stray dog really came from? This is a story about just such a dog.

Demon Dog
by Joy Ward

I am Seamus and I am a demon. Or am I a dog?

Let me back up to the beginning. Oh. Not the beginning of my existence as a demon. That was thousands of years ago and frankly, I don't really remember all the particulars. That story has been told elsewhere. No, the story I'm going to tell you is how I became a dog and what came after.

It was a cold, windy day when my boss – a much stronger and well placed demon than me—called me into his throne room. Of course I dropped my broom (I had been sweeping out the grand hallway) and ran to answer my boss. His throne room isn't as large as The Lightbringer's Big Room but it's really shiny in its own right. The boss's throne room is about fifty feet by a hundred feet with an arched foyer leading into it. No rugs but, whew, those golden floors are mighty nice! The light from the ornate golden candleholders spaced about every ten feet along the walls. Then there's the boss's golden high throne set with cut crystals… Like I said, shiny!

When I got there I found the boss already had some company. Three demon gents I didn't know stood or sat near the throne, apparently in deep conversation with the boss. They had the usual demon look to them—like handsome human men two of whom had dark hair touching their shirt collars and the third kind of blonde with a shorter do. All three were dressed in fairly modern jeans and t-shirts. I went through the door way and waited about twenty feel in front of the throne waiting for my boss to call me forward or tell me what he wanted me to get him.

The boss looked up and right at me. His deep chestnut hair mirrored by the forked beard and matching mustache that begged to be twirled at the end. The Boss's deep-set brown eyes reminded me of dark pools at the bottom of old wells. He wore a russet brown silk shirt with black silk breeches.

The three unknown demons turned around and also looked my way. I knew how a pinned moth felt being scrutinized by a kid.

"Do you gents need anything? Anything I can do for you, Boss?" I dropped a quick half bow and waited.

"Seamus, come here." My boss gestured me over to them and pointed at a spot a few feet away, next to one of the dark-haired demons. He smiled slightly. Now I'm all for being in the good graces of my higher-ups but my boss's smile is enough to make my blood run backwards on a good day. On a day like today when I have no idea what he wants, well, let me say I was glad I still was out of his arm's length. I dropped another half bow just for good measure.

"So this is the young demon you want to send undercover?" The dark haired demon next to me growled. I noticed his Celtic Bagpipes t-shirt had a rather nasty brownish stain near the edge of one sleeve cuff. Rather not look at that.

"Yes. Seamus here is quite faithful and uh, follows orders. He should fit what you want." My boss smiled again, still not reassuring me. In fact, I distinctly did not like the way these gents were eyeing me. I had the feeling they eyed tasty baked goods the same way. It occurred to me if I stood still maybe they would forget I was there. Just thinking…

At that point the blonde spoke up, in a definitely higher pitch than his fellow's. "Do you think he can manage this? He doesn't look like much."

I wasn't sure what to make of that. I felt my bright red skin flare a darker red and my already red eyes flash just a bit. I couldn't afford to get mad at them and I knew better than to let them see any anger. Hell's hierarchy was not kind to demons like me who stood up to my betters. So I bucked up and stood completely still. I learned a long time ago to hold my forked tongue.

"Seamus, these men are officials from the Subterfuge Committee. They have asked me for a volunteer for a very particular job above ground and I have volunteered you." His smile became bigger and scarier.

"Um, yes sir. Whatever you say, sir." I made a thorough study of the boss' very nice footwear but I could still feel his and the other demons' eyes on me. I swallowed hard.

The third demon grumbled. "I don't know, he looks pretty weak and spindly. And look at that potbelly. Is he to be a pig or a dpg? Do you think the woman will take him?" He wiped his paws on his blue shirt and stuck them in his jean pockets.

"She's on the Other Side. How bright can she be?" The blonde spit out and chortled.

The first dark-haired demon harrumphed. "He's what we've got."

That decided my fate.

The next thing I knew the three demons whisked me away to a small room I had never seen. We sat around an oblong wood table and they proceeded to fill me in on my mission. I was to be turned into a physical dog and worm my way into the home of a couple who were causing Down Below some trouble. The couple, Homer and Lilah, were keeping their area quite positive even against Underworld's best attempts to tear up their area. Even worse than that, the couple had strong angelic connections and had cancelled out Underworld's efforts with those connections. We had to neutralize them or we could not make inroads into this part of the planet.

The Subterfuge Committee had come up with the idea that one of us would sneak into her home and report when she acted, and stuff. The only way to do that was as a dog because the humans wouldn't accept a strange human without a complete spiritual check. None of our usual suspects could gain the confidence of the woman and her husband. But the couple did rescue dogs.

"How long will this take, gents? I have duties down here that must be…" I began to ask the three over-demons when the blonde gave me a backhand cuff to quiet me.

"Not to worry, squirt. Someone else can do your sweeping." The blonde made a sound that reminded me of laughing.

There was that. This mission would take me out of Underworld and away from the bullies who were rife among the demon hordes. It seemed I never got to finish even a small meal without somebody grabbing my plate from me. Maybe I would even get to sleep longer than an hour without somebody tossing me out of my rag bed for fun. If I did well, maybe I could move up the ranks where I could have a real bed! That would be marvelous!

The trio shape shifted me into my dog body; barrel body, red like me with a long white-tipped tail, red eyes and a rather attractive freckling on my otherwise white chest and paws. I thought I was quite the looker! While I got used to my over-sized paws and the fact that my spine ended in a tail, the three demons explained to me that my duty was to let them know anytime the woman or the husband did anything suspicious. I nodded accordingly but my language was sadly limited.

After an hour or so of background on the human couple and the spiritual front they were defending, Celtic Bagpipe guy showed up with a long length of yellow police tape that said "keep out! Do not cross!" He reached out and attached it to my collar.

I gave him a quizzical look since I was still missing a facility for language.

"You have to have a leash for the demon agent to lead you. Otherwise, it will look suspicious if you just show up." Celtic pipes gent looked quite pleased with himself. "This was my idea."

The next thing I knew I was standing in a parking lot behind some stores with another demon in the shape of a young woman. It was cold enough this afternoon she was shivering in her human form as she held the end of the ersatz leash in her right hand.

I obviously couldn't ask her the next thing for me so I waited and sniffed the air. Amazing nose I had! As a demon I didn't have that great a sniffer but hoo boy! As a dog I could smell everything! Maybe this wasn't going to be so bad.

The demon holding my leash had been standing in one place for maybe five minutes when I felt her tense up. She whispered, "Here they come. Seamus. Cute up!"

The couple, a man and a woman, stopped by a grey car as he fumbled with pulling his keys out of his jeans. Leash demon walked toward them, looking slightly frazzled. The middle-aged roundish woman turned toward us, saw me and smiled.

Bingo! She liked me!

The demon moved the leash from hand to the other, pulling her brown marled sweater closer across her chest. "I'm sorry for bothering you but do you know this dog? He wandered into my shop over there and I don't know what to do with him."

The middle-aged man in a grey wool sweater looked concerned. "No, he's not one of ours. Maybe he got out of is yard or off his leash."

"Do you know how to get him into a shelter or rescue?"

"Of course," the man began, you..."

My demon handler did not give him space for another word as she literally threw the yellow paper leash at the woman, who was closest to her. "I have to get back to my shop. Thank you." By the time the woman looked back up my demon handler had disappeared. The couple looked at each other and laughed. Laughed! Then the woman opened the car door and urged me in.

Didn't have to ask me twice!

I thought to myself that was nicely done. Either I was cuter than I thought or these two were not very bright. Either way, I was in their car in fewer than five minutes. Score one for the Subterfuge Committee!

The man drove us back to their house where I was met by a big surprise—other dogs! Nobody told me I would have to get through other dogs. This made everything so much more complicated. The humans didn't recognize me but the dogs would. And they did. The five dogs, ranging in size from about forty to a hundred pounds, met us at the wooden gate ready to sniff my butt and defend their yard.

The five dogs were not happy to see me. None of them wanted to let me in their yard. The three Weimaraners formed a substantial backfield while the black Lab mix and the Beagle were the first to confront me. All five of the dogs surrounded me, sniffing and voicing their concerns. Not only could I not speak any human language I couldn't even speak dog. Somebody did not think this through.

I couldn't tell what the dogs were saying but I could tell it was not, "let's throw the new kid a party." I got the distinct impression they had figured out I was not like them. The way the alpha, a big male Weimaraner, looked at me I suspected he knew what I was.

Fortunately, I smelled like a dog and that helped, maybe.

The Subterfuge Committee had planned ahead enough to give me a thing called a "chip" so when Homer took me to the veterinarian (don't ask but it was terrible) the machine told them my name was Seamus.

Meanwhile, Lilah seemed to not understand why the other dogs did not like me. So she made a point with the home pack that they were to accept me no matter what. I remember that time because it was the first time anybody ever wanted to accept me.

It was the first afternoon when I arrived. Homer and Lilah brought me into their home and made all the dogs back away from me and sit down. How kind was that! Even as demon kid nobody ever made a fuss over me like they did. Back in the kid demon den I had just been one of a hundred or so and nobody much cared what you did as long as you did not cause trouble.

Homer and Lilah tied a yellow bandana around my neck, had me sit between them on their dark leather sofa and called over each dog one by one to be introduced. Homer would pet me and Lilah would pet the other dog, or the reverse depending on where the other dog stood. None of the other dogs were thrilled but they followed their human alphas. I learned later that they did that because the humans loved them, not because the dogs were afraid of them.

Meanwhile, I soaked up the petting! OOO, that was my first time to feel that, too. Feeling Homer or Lilah's hands run down my back was like nothing I ever felt before. I could have sat there all night just for those pets! And wagging my long red, white-tipped tail was so much fun!

When we were all introduced, Lilah gave us a little lecture about being pack. "We love all of you. Seamus is just a puppy and needs us right now. We are going to try to find his people but we need you to help." Most of the dogs understood her but still were not too happy about having a demon in their midst. One of them, a big, old Weimaraner named Sarge, came up next to me, actually shoving me. He said something but I couldn't understand dog yet. I found out later he was telling me he was watching me. The hundred pound grey dog knew what I was and was not happy about having me there.

So I settled in the three story house. It was comfortable with colorful throw rugs in each room and doggy beds in most of the rooms. During the day the sun shone through the high windows. I took the time to walk around on my big feet and get used to being a four-footed instead of a two-footed. It was harder to see things being as short as I was but every chance I got I climbed up on one of the leather couches or chairs to get a better view.

The second night, the black Lab mix, Jersey, barked an alarm in the back yard. I knew it was probably some demon from the Committee checking on me. I couldn't tell the home pack to not worry. So they all poured out the doggy door set in the white wooden back door to bark at whatever was out there.

 I was the last out the door so by the time I got to the yard everybody else had already taken their places for defense. The clear night sky made it easy to smell the demon hanging around the alley behind the house. All the other dogs barked and prepared to do battle so there wasn't too much for me to do except wait. It wasn't long before the demon, one I didn't recognize, realized he couldn't get through eh wards and left. When the demon left, everybody filed back in and flopped down on a doggy bed or a piece of furniture. The warm house lulled me into a dream of me as a dog chasing squirrels. Odd, I'd never had a dream like that before.

The next morning I woke up on a red and blue striped doggy bed with my paws straight up in the air. Clangs of metal bowls in the black and white tiled kitchen announced breakfast. I realized I could better understand what the other dogs were saying to each other.

I guess the dog body had started to claim me because I couldn't wait for Homer and Lilah to dole out breakfast, some tasty kibble. Homer made sure I got a fair share and nobody took my aluminum bowl away from me. How different from down below where only the swift and the strong ate well!"

Sarge still didn't like me and let me know it. He made a point of shoving me with his hundred plus pound body when he got close enough. "Puppy, I think not! You have the smell of demon all over you, red one. Try to hurt the Mama or the Daddy and I'll be so far down your throat I'll find a ball I lost last year." Then he sauntered to the other side of the room, planted his huge paws and stared at me with his dark gold eyes.

He was not going to make this easy.

A few days went by before the demon watcher came back. During that time, I got to cuddle with the Mama and the Daddy! How marvelous! We sat on the black leather couch watching the TV. I'd seen these before but the combination of cuddles and watching the pictures was, dare I say it, heavenly!

It was late at night when I felt the demon out back, unable to get past the salt and wards my family had put up and maintained. I only got through because the Mama and the Daddy brought me through with them. Otherwise I would have been stuck on the other side of the fence.

"Seamus! Demon Seamus. Get out here." It was the demon who had been wearing the celtic pipes t-shirt. "Seamus, come report to me."

It was late enough that everyone else had settled into sleep. I ran out the doggy door into the cold night and down the wooden stairs before the other dogs could hear him and sound the alarm. "I'm here. What do you want? Please be quieter or the other dogs will hear you." I was aware of the squirrel in the big oak tree next to the path. I could almost hear her warning the other squirrels about the demon at the gate.

"Other dogs, what do you mean other dogs? You aren't a dog, Seamus. You're a demon and don't forget that." He stood as close to the wood gate as he could and hissed at me. "What can you tell us? What are the humans up to? Does the female call on her angelic connections? Speak quickly, demon!"

"There is nothing to report, lord demon. No angels, no activity."

"Have the dogs identified you? Should we pull you out now?"

The demon's words scared me. I didn't want to leave this place where I had cuddles and lots of food. All the other dogs did not really like me but the Mama and the Daddy did. No, I wanted to stay. "No, sir, I should stay here and keep watching them. It has only been a short time and something may happen I should report."

"For now you stay, demon." With that he disappeared with a whiff of sulpher.

"Hachoo!" I sneezed as it went up my much better nose.

A few weeks passed, with me becoming more and more comfortable in this place. I even began to think of it as home and this, maybe, my pack. I loved being a dog! No sweeping. No fighting for food. Here someone even showed me affection! Besides, I had this marvelous red nose and long soft ears that the Mama and the Daddy liked to pet. The other dogs had begun to get used to me, even assigning me a position in the pack when we went into defensive measures. For the first time in my thousands of years alive I had found a place where I could be accepted and maybe even loved. No, I did not want to go back to being a demon.

Then one night it happened. An angel showed up in the house. It was Michael! I'd only heard about him but he knew me on sight. He called me to the back yard, away from the humans. The dogs heard us, though, and came out to form a silent audience.

"Little Seamus, what are you?" Michael stood tall before me, radiating strength. I could not lie to those burning blue eyes. His dark curls hugged his head as the chilly air softly swirled around him. I couldn't see his sword but I could feel it behind him.

"I don't know, Archangel. I began as a demon, as you know, but things have changed." I scuffed the ground in front of me with my right paw. In the light of the moon my paw freckles stood out from the white fur.

His voice, steel strong overlaid with a velvet coverlet, seemed to reach into my bones. "Who do you serve, little one?"

"I, I don't know. I never knew anyone could accept me." I was so confused. Michael had not vanquished me. I was still a dog and had not been sent back to Underworld. "I really like these humans. I want to stay but if I don't go back The Boss will make me suffer for it…"

"The choice is yours, little one." With that, the Archangel disappeared into the night air.

The clear night sky crackled with dark energy as five demons appeared on the other side of the gate, prepared for battle. The other dogs leaped into action, taking their defensive positions along the fence and in front of the house. I felt several angels appear on the building's roof.

"Seamus, to your position!" Nigel, the alpha Weimaraner, urged me to "a spot next to him as the dogs prepared to stand with the angelic hosts. He barked out orders to the other dogs.

"Yes, Alpha!" I proudly stood next to him against the demons. I was accepted and one of them. I would not give that up!

The battle was quick but how other humans could not see the battle I have no idea.

The demon I knew as my watcher, celtic pipes guy, was one of the five. He saw me and demanded I help them. "Seamus, I am calling you to work with us NOW! If you do not, you will be banned from Underworld!" He flashed a huge sword that shone with a blackish gleam.

The other four demons seemed to be under him, waiting for his orders. The three demons were in various stages of losing their human disguises. Their faces strobed between looking like young males and faces that looked like gila monsters, mottled green and brown. Their arms likewise flashed back and forth between mostly human and brownish green scales. Only celtic pipes guy was high-ranking enough to have black wings sprouting from his back. The others must not have earned theirs yet.

"All of you, over that fence now! Neutralize the humans!" With that the leader made the first run at the wards. The others followed close behind him.

All five hit the wards which barely held. A loud sizzle resounded across the yard. The demons pulled back but for only a moment.

The front line of dogs hit the fence, hard! They snarled their challenges to the demons on the other side of the wards.

The next charge took the demons through the wards and into the yard, where they were met with white beams of energy from Homer and Lilah. The white light flared into almost blinding brightness as it hit the Underworlders. Two of the demons were flung out of the yard, maybe all the way to Underworld. The smell of steamed demon made two of the dogs sneeze.

That left three demons, celtic pipes and two lesser ones. Nigel, the alpha Weim got celtic pipes by his upper left rear thigh where the demon couldn't hit him with his sword. Then another Weim, Daisy, took her cue and grabbed the demon at the rear of the other thigh and got her share of demon blood. I could hear the two dogs complaining about how bad his blood tasted but they held on in hopes of getting a souvenir. The scene was so comical I had to stop and look. Wow, if Underworld could see him now… I only had a moment to enjoy his discomfort before I was called back to the battle.

Jersey, the Lab, and the third Weim, Sarge, both each had a leg of one of the other demons and were working on a wishbone maneuver. The third demon was locked in an energy battle with Lilah and Homer.

I harried the two demons so they couldn't get a clear bead on the pack. The hunt excitement drew me in and for a few minutes I forgot I wasn't a dog!

Lilah and Homer vanquished the third demon and I felt a "pop" as the air closed around where he had been. Back to Underworld for him.

About this time I saw several white flashes and four angles appeared, Michael among them. The two demons currently being treated as tug toys, quickly escaped. Our jaws clapped close. I thought I might have loosened a tooth or two but I would have to worry about that later.

The angels left a guard but we dogs went back inside. We all found soft spots. Beatrice the beagle lay down next to me, something she had never done. "So you have chosen a side, one-who –was-once-a-demon. Did you think we did not know?" Her own freckled paws touched mine on the doggy bed. "Are you now a dog with us?"

"I guess so. No, I am proud to be accepted by you and the rest of the pack if you will have me." My heart beat a little faster in my red barrel of a chest. I could still taste demon blood in my mouth.

"We all have pasts. The Mama and the Daddy have accepted us. How can we not offer you the same forgiveness?" Then she put her soft white head down and closed her eyes.

I noticed the other four dogs were watching us. They sent me the message that they knew what Beatrice had offered me and agreed with her. Even Sarge. I could feel my red tail thumping on the wood floor behind me. Is this happiness? I had never known happiness but I knew this had to be it!

My life as a dog would be shorter but I could not give up this feeling of "pack" and love for a thousand more years as a demon.

I am Seamus and I am a dog!

Walt Boyes has been owned by Corgis for many years. This story combines Corgi's' Celtic mysticism with Southwestern myth to show us primates how canids work together. It first appeared in Everything Corgi.

Bluebonnet Jillie

by Walt Boyes

Suddenly Jillie sat up straight, wide-awake. Her upright prick ears twitched back and forth like radar. Her nose sniffed the breeze. Something was strange. She looked at the sky, but she could see nothing out of place. It was a nice, clear day. The sky was high, and blue, with just a few raggedy white clouds. The sun was very warm.

She had been snoozing and dreaming. It was a very warm late spring day in Central Texas, and there wasn't much for a Pembroke Welsh Corgi to do but dream of sheep and cows and running after them. Jillie was a red and white dog, with dark red fur that was a little more curly than it should have been for a show dog. She'd been in a kennel fight when she was younger, and she had two divots in her skull that made her head a little pointy, and made it hard to close her mouth all the way. She smiled a lot.

She'd been making little barking noises under her breath, and her feet were jerking a little as if she were running while she was lying down. She dreamed of sheep and cows because she was a Corgi, and those were some of a Corgi's favorite things. She was a herding dog, and Corgis love to run after sheep and cows to make them go where they are supposed to go.

It was even possible that she'd been dreaming of herding magical sheep for her Faery friends. Corgis come from Wales, you see, which is one of the ways to get to the land of Faery, located east of the Sun and west of the Moon.

The inhabitants of Faery use corgis as their magical steeds because Corgis are very short, and are often born with a saddle-like marking. Although Jillie lived in the Texas Hill Country with her girl, Andrea, the magic was strong in her and she often had adventures.

Jillie was just thinking about circling around three times, nose to tailbone, and curling up again to sleep, when she sensed it again. Jillie wasn't dreaming any more.

Something was wrong in the field behind the house. Something was very wrong. Jillie sat very still and then slowly looked around.

Laddybuck, the younger Corgi who had come into the family to learn how to be a dog, didn't even twitch. Typical, Jillie sighed. He was so sound asleep he wasn't moving much, except to breathe. He had been chasing the water coming out of the rotating lawn sprinkler all morning, and he had run about a hundred miles in a big circle, barking and biting at the water as it squirted. Laddybuck was a sable Corgi, with black pointed ears, and black on his muzzle. He had the right coat, and good conformation, but he was goofy, and didn't have the concentration to be a show dog. That's why he'd come to live with Andrea and Jillie.

Jillie snorted. He wouldn't be of much help.

Andrea was swinging on her swing set in the other corner of the back yard. It was a small back yard, with a big covered wooden deck, big bushes, some roses, and a huge metal swing set for Andrea. The swing set was rusty in spots, and the swing squeaked when it moved. Up, squeak. Down, squeak. Up. Down. Nothing wrong there.

Jillie stood up. She shook herself. She started at her nose, and the shake moved up her red head to her neck, past the white blaze, and down the wavy red fur of her back to her back end where she had no tail. Her whole posterior moved back and forth, and then the shake moved back toward her head and finished at her nose again.

Jillie was getting a little older, and she had a trace of arthritis, so she gingerly moved down the steps of the deck to the lawn. She slowly paced over the lawn to the fence, and her diggy hole. All dogs have diggy holes. Jillie's was a way to get under the fence and out of the yard whenever she wanted to. Andrea's father was not in favor of diggy holes, and he kept filling it in. This time he'd put a couple of big rocks on top of the dirt in front of the fence.

Jillie knew what to do. She put her nose between the rocks and pushed. The rocks rolled apart enough for her to get her paw between them. She dragged the rocks away from her diggy hole, went back and began to dig.

She didn't have to dig a very big hole, because she could make herself very small and thin, and slip under the fence. There's debate about whether that is a magical skill or whether all dogs have it. It was also very useful for hiding behind the couch if she had done something bad. Jillie smiled to herself as she remembered the time she had stolen the whole package of hamburger out of the shopping bag and hidden and eaten it all.

At any rate, Jillie quickly popped her head, and then the rest of her, out on the other side of the fence. And just like that, she was trotting down the sidewalk to the end of the street.

Just as though she was supposed to be there, Jillie nodded to the neighbors as she passed them on the sidewalk. There was Guitar Man, who lived next door, and the Gardening Lady, who had ten green thumbs. And there was the nice lady whose daughter was Andrea's best friend. They all smiled and waved, and Jillie smiled back, tongue lolling out of her mouth a little as she trotted toward the field.

As soon as she passed Gardening Lady's house, Jillie stepped off the sidewalk into the field. The field was high with weeds and flowers. It was colorful and beautiful. It was still springtime. In Texas, springtime means wildflowers. There are hundreds of kinds and colors. And there are bluebonnets, tall stalks with dozens of little bell-shaped blue flowers on them. In Texas, the bluebonnets are beautiful and important, because they signal the coming of spring. In addition, in Texas, bluebonnets grow everywhere.

The bluebonnets were especially lovely in the field behind Jillie's house. There were whole patches of nothing but bluebonnets. Andrea's parents would dress her in a very pretty dress and plop her down in the middle of the biggest bluebonnet patch they could find and take pictures of her every year. Sometimes they made Jillie lie down in the bluebonnet patch and take pictures of her, too. They said that the combination of Jillie's russet coat and the blue flowers made wonderful pictures.

Jillie stopped and nosed the bluebonnet patch, warily. No, the problem wasn't on the bluebonnets. Whatever she was feeling, it wasn't them.

Jillie moved quickly and quietly through the field. She went wide around one patch of very thick weeds, because she knew that was where the rattlesnake lived. She went around another patch because she had gotten in trouble just the other day for trying to chase Mrs. Bunny and her babies, who lived in the weeds in the middle of the field.

Then she saw the trouble. It looked like a dog, but it wasn't. It was long and skinny, with gray and tan fur, very long legs and a low, bushy tail. Its face was sharp, with prick ears like a Corgi's, and sharp fangs, too. The air around it was shimmery like a rainbow. One minute it wasn't there, and the next it was. The creature was growling and snarling right at Jillie!

Jillie backed away, a low rumble in her throat. She barked her low, raspy bark, and the not-dog looked sharply at her. As it turned, she recognized it. It was a coyote. Since it had appeared by magic, it must be a magic coyote. Jillie had heard about the magical coyotes of the Native Americans, but she had never seen one.

She must be very close to the Double File Trail, she thought to herself.

Long before the settlers from the South and East moved into Texas, many other people had lived there in their turns. There was an old trail, just wide enough for two people to walk side by side, that ran South to North in Texas, and it was called the Double File Trail.

When she had first come to live with Andrea and Laddybuck, Jillie had discovered that the Double File Trail was a way into the land of Faery. Over the years, she had visited the land of Faery many times, and had some strange adventures there. However, she had never visited the part of Faery where the magical creatures of the Native Americans lived.

The coyote stopped growling. He cocked his head to one side. He grinned a coyote grin, as if he was apologizing for growling at Jillie. He wagged his long, bushy tail. He smiled a sort of sharp, toothy smile. He moved a step toward Jillie. She stopped backing away. She also smiled a sharp, toothy smile. She wanted him to know that she was a tough and magical Corgi. She just loved to keep not-dogs like him away from sheep and small girls and the other members of her flock.

Slowly, Jillie and the coyote came closer to each other. Finally, they touched noses, tall nose to short one. They sniffed. They sniffed down each other's flank, and sniffed each other's rears like dogs and wolves and coyotes do. They made friends.

The coyote made a movement that told Jillie he wanted her to follow him. He lowered his head, stretched out his front paws and bounced into the air, turning around as he leaped. As he turned, a path appeared that hadn't been there a moment before. He stepped onto the path and trotted up it a short way, turned, and looked at Jillie, expectantly. He panted a little, to show he was waiting.

Jillie thought, and then she made up her mind. She trotted up the path after him. In the field behind her, the path disappeared. They trotted side by side through a field full of bluebonnets, Indian Paintbrush, Mexican Hats, and the other spring wildflowers of Texas. Jillie could hear the birds, and here and there, a cicada chirping. Coyote set a fast pace, and Jillie found herself working hard to keep up with him, since his legs were so much longer than hers.

Every few hundred yards, there was a big oak tree, all by itself, with a few cactus plants around under the drip line. Coyote excused himself politely, once, and went and did his business under one of the oaks. Jillie waited, and when he came back, they went on up the trail again. Coyote seemed to know where he was going. Jillie thought she would just tag along and see what happened. He seemed nice enough, for a magical Coyote.

It got later and later, and finally Coyote found a place to sleep, just off the trail under one of the huge oak trees. Jillie excused herself and went behind the oak tree to do her business. When she came back, she saw Coyote turning three times in his own length and curling up in the shadow of the tree. She curled up next to him, and before she knew it, they were both asleep.

The next morning, Jillie and Coyote started back up the Double File Trail. They trotted together silently again for a long time.

Finally, Jillie and Coyote came to a river. There were high bluffs overlooking the river, and the path curved around the bluffs and down to the river edge. At first, Jillie thought they were going to swim across the river, but she saw Coyote sniffing round the base of the bluffs. He found a small cave in the bluff at the very edge of the river. He hesitated a moment, and then he went inside the cave. Jillie followed. Inside the cave it was dim, but not dark. Light filtered down from above somewhere. Coyote padded on the sandy cave floor toward the back of the cave. Again, Jillie was right behind him. The cave narrowed until it became a passageway. It never got completely dark, but there were times when Jillie kept moving forward because she could smell Coyote in front of her better than she could see him.

Suddenly, Coyote stopped so suddenly that his big bushy tail slapped Jillie in the face. She yelped quietly. She moved forward so she was standing next to Coyote. They were at the end of the passage. In front of them was a large cavern. It was big enough to have its own clouds, and it had trees, plants, and lots of people all huddled together.

There were some very strange looking creatures moving around in the cavern, getting closer and closer to the people. They were long-backed, black and brown, with very long scaly tails, and had very large teeth and very long claws. The people were obviously afraid of them. The creatures were snarling, snapping, and trying to grab the people and drag them into the shadows. Some of the people had sticks and were using them to hit the creatures.

Coyote looked at Jillie, as if to say,

"See why I came and got you?"

 Jillie knew what to do. There were people in her flock. These were people. So they must be in her flock, too. She was a brave Corgi, and she wasn't going to let any nasty creatures get her people.

She charged between the people and the creatures, barking and snapping. Her eyes flashed. Her bunny butt hugged the ground as she sprang at the creatures. They backed up, startled.

The people were shouting. Behind Jillie, Coyote had started to change his form. His outline shimmered and flowed into the shape of a human woman, dressed in a long buckskin dress that was covered with beading in beautiful designs. His shape grew until he had become a very big woman indeed, and able to touch the roof of the cavern, above the clouds. The Changing Woman punched her hand into the roof and made a hole large enough for her to grow bigger.

She enlarged the hole, and then she reached down, and picked up one of the people and carried it up out of the cavern.

The nasty creatures became very angry when they saw this. Jillie understood that it was going to be her job to keep the creatures away from the people while the Changing Woman, who used to be Coyote, carried them up out of the cave.

The Changing Woman kept carrying the people up out of the cavern, and Jillie kept charging and snapping at the ugly creatures.

She dodged their claws as they tried to grab her. Not one of them laid a paw on her. She dodged, ducked and turned, just like she would do as if she were herding sheep in Wales. Finally all the people were out of the cave, and the Changing Woman reached down and picked up Jillie in her huge hand. She raised her hand until Jillie, too, was out of the cave. The shape of the Changing Woman flowed upward too, and with a last wave of her hand, she sealed the entrance to the cavern below. As the cavern sealed, the Changing Woman slowly changed back into Jillie's friend, Coyote. He sat there, tongue lolling, and laughing in his Coyote way. Jillie barked back, and smiled her sharp, toothy Corgi smile. She felt good. She had kept her flock safe.

They were very far from Texas, Jillie saw. They were in a place where it was very dry. The sun was hot, and there were very tall mountains in the distance with snow on them. Jillie knew that there were no mountains like that in the Texas Hill Country. She knew snow when she saw it, though, because it had once snowed at the house she lived in with Andrea and for a few hours the back yard was covered with the cold icky white stuff. Laddybuck, of course, had loved it and kept yapping and running and jumping in it. It figured.

There were some very tall bluffs across the valley from where they stood on a wide mesa, and the people pointed to the cave openings they could see. Jillie could still not understand what they were saying, but it was clear that the people thought they would have a safe new home here.

Coyote looked at the people, and then he looked at Jillie. Silently, they backed away from the people, and trotted off down the path they found leading off the mesa. They trotted side-by-side for a while, big Coyote and short Jillie. It wasn't long, though, before the trail started to look a lot like Texas. Coyote seemed to know where he was going, and after a while, Jillie thought she knew where they were going, too.

Soon the field that the trail ran through looked a lot like the field behind Andrea's house. Coyote stopped at a branch path. He nudged Jillie with his muzzle. He licked the side of her face. Then he turned and ran up the trail without stopping and without looking back. Jillie stood watching him until she couldn't see him any more. Then she headed down the branch trail into the field behind Andrea's house.

She was very far off in the field. She was on the other side of the creek, and she could just barely see Andrea's street and the houses in the gaps in the trees that lined the bed of the creek.

She headed toward the wooden footbridge over the creek toward home. She was suddenly very tired, and looking forward to being home.

*There is nothing sweeter than a senior human and a
senior dog caring for each other...even to the end.*

Last Walk

By Joy Ward

This story is about love, love that carries through death.
Oh, it's not a story about romantic love. There are plenty
of those. This is a story about an unselfish love. This is a
story about love that accepts unconditionally and asks
for nothing. This is a story about the love between a
rescuer and the last dogs she saves.

Margaret was an old woman who loved dogs. She loved
big dogs and small dogs, short-haired dogs and long-
haired dogs, quiet dogs and not-so-quiet dogs. She loved
puppies, too. But what Margaret loved the most were
old dogs. You know, the ones who sleep a lot and
maybe can't see so well any more. They're the ones who
hang back when the treats and pets are being given out
because they have a little arthritis or aren't so sure on
their legs. They don't want the other dogs to bump them
or even knock them over. They're the dogs who might
have trouble eating hard food but try any way. You
know those dogs.

Some people want puppies or young dogs with strong
legs to go up stairs or jump on beds. Margaret loved
those dogs too. But, maybe because Margaret was old or
maybe because she was just such a caring person, she
had a soft spot for old dogs. She used to say that she fit
right in with them. She said they were her speed, slow.

Then she'd laugh and pet the nearest fuzzy back. And there were always plenty of fuzzy backs to pet.

Margaret would say, "We get along cause I'm old, too." Then she'd give that throaty laugh and pet another dog. Of course, she had been saying that for so long she must have started taking care of old dogs long before she really was old.

Before I go any further let me tell you about Margaret. She had been my neighbor for as long as I had lived in my home. That would be over twenty years or so. Margaret was one of those people who seemed to slip between fifteen and her actual age of eighty-nine. One minute se was the serious crone overseeing her canine kingdom and the next something shifted around her and you could swear she was a teenage girl playing fetch with another new-old dog. She had long blonde hair that had faded more to a very light blonde rather than outright grey or white. It was almost like even Nature was trying to treat her with unusual respect. So Nature touched Margaret the way she touched her elder charges, with love.

Margaret wasn't a particularly small or large woman. She was somewhere between five foot and five foot four depending on how she felt that day. She had a bit of arthritis in her back so some days she might not stand as tall. She usually wore comfortable jeans with the occasional stain on the knees or calves. Her shirts were roomy but slightly tailored and almost always pullovers. She almost always smelled like lavender, her favorite flower.

People always remembered Margaret. There was just something about Margaret that made people remember her. She had a way of making everyone feel relaxed in her presence.

Margaret had been a teacher, a professor in fact, before she retired. She taught anthropology. When she retired she left that all behind and I rarely heard her bring up the topic except to mention dogs in history.

After she was gone people would recount this story or that about Margaret but the one thing they always remembered was her love for dogs, all dogs, but especially old dogs. She always said, "Every old dog has been there for some human. We should be there for them" She asserted that there was a covenant between dogs and humans. Dogs lived up to their side and Margaret said taking care of dogs when they get old is part of living up to our side.

So Margaret took care of old dogs.

I have no idea how many old dogs she rescued. She was the last resort for old dogs being tossed into an early death by circumstances or uncaring humans. She took in dogs whose humans had died and had not made arrangements for the dogs they left behind. She adopted dogs whose humans had fallen into assisted care and mental wards. Then there were the dogs who were tossed out by their humans because the dogs were older and a little more trouble. Those were the ones that made Margaret the angriest because they were preventable. Margaret could get pretty riled up about abuse cases but I think these "dog dumps" as she called them made her the maddest. "How stupid or unfeeling do you have to be to throw out a perfectly good dog just because he gets a little slower or she gets a little leakier? I hope these idiots get treated exactly the same way when they get older. What kind of example do they think they're setting for their children? Mom and Dad get to be a bit of trouble so you can toss them out?" Then she would get back to tending to her old dogs. There was always another diaper to change or special food to mix. But Margaret didn't seem to mind. I think every time she got tired she's just pet another dog and remind herself what they had lost.

She never seemed to mind cleaning up after them, either. I know she always had another load of laundry to do or another pill to give. That was okay. She would clean up whatever mess was there and then pull up a high-backed Victorian seat next to her huge front window and brush down another old dog as she watched the world roll by outside.

Someone asked her once if rescuing older dogs was depressing. Puppies and younger dogs usually move on to forever homes but older dogs won't find new homes. Margaret knew that when she took in an old dog that dog would probably die in her home. In effect, Margaret ran an old dog hospice. She was the last stop before they moved into death. Many of them were in good health but the hard fact was that too few people wanted to give them a chance. Most people want a young dog so they don't have to face death any sooner than necessary.

The last time someone asked her that question Margaret let loose a short laugh and gave the young, dark-haired woman a long look. "Are you afraid of death? Is it something to hide from or avoid seeing? It's as much a part of life as breathing or being born. All things die. What a coward I would be to not help these senior citizens because I didn't want to face death! I miss them when they leave but I treasure the time I can spend with them before the end. I learn so much from them! Yes, it is sad for me when they die but I love knowing that I made their last days or years happy. Sad, yes, but depressing? No."

When the weather was nice Margaret would put all the dogs who could walk easily into harnesses and take them out. They made a motley parade making its way slowly down the avenue. Her retinue could include a Great Dane with its long arthritic legs and a white-muzzled Weimaraner with cataracts gingerly feeling her way along next to an ancient Brittney. The breeds varied and changed as the elderly canines passed into eternity and other dogs took their places in Margaret's canine hospice.

So for more years than I can guess Margaret was the last home for dogs with no one else. Untold numbers of dogs spent their last days with Margaret and she never flinched from holding their paws as they passed from one world to the next.

Margaret always said death was the one thing we all had to meet alone but she could help her "sweet ones" to the edge and give them what comfort she could until they went beyond her touch. When they passed, Margaret made sure each body was treated with love and respect, either buried or cremated and the ashes spread over her mildly unkempt large yard. She didn't keep all the ashes but she did keep a framed picture of each and every dog who had been with her. Each photo had the dog's name and year he or she died clearly engraved on the frame. At least twenty or thirty of these portraits were arrayed on a bamboo bookshelf in her eclectic living room. Another twenty or so hung in her long hallway. She never forgot any of her canine charges. And they never forgot her, either.

Did Margaret ever talk about her own death? Only to say that she expected to see her "sweet ones" again. I honestly don't think death was something she feared. Maybe she had spent too much time with Death as she watched Him embrace her old babies to fear him. Death had become if not a friend, then at least a close acquaintance.

The only thing she worried about was dying and leaving a dog or four behind. She knew what happened to dogs left with no one to love them and she did not want to do that to one of hers. But what could she do? She could have stopped rescuing old dogs but that was not part of her plan. She had to help as many as she could.

When I asked her what would happen with the dogs she left behind when she went through the Dark Door she said not to worry. "Maybe we'll all go together or maybe some of my babies who have gone before will come back to help us join them." Then she would laugh and change the subject.

The last time I saw Margaret she was on one of her daily walks with an assortment of older, blinder and somewhat lamer dogs. There was a grizzled Black Labrador Retriever with a white muzzle. There was a fat, long in the tooth Beagle boy and an Aussie mix with eyes that could barely see much beyond shadows. A proud ancient Shih Tzu led the stroll, his nails making a faint click-click as he maintained his forward watch. She had maybe ten or twelve dogs with her. I recognized a few of the dogs as current adoptees. But there was something about the others that tickled the back of my mind. There was something I should have seen but didn't. The afternoon sun warmed the dogs and Margaret as they made their way together westward, their old pack standing together against the world.

Most days Margaret looked and felt like a mountain that time passed by. But not that day. That day, Margaret looked older, weaker. I asked her how she felt and of course she said she was fine. What else would Margaret say? She rarely complained or asked for help for herself so what could I do? I let her pass by and the next time I saw her, well, things had changed.

I stopped her for a moment but the dogs seemed anxious to move on. The Lab tugged at his harness. Margaret gave a knowing smile and reassured him they would be moving soon. "Max, there is plenty of time to get where we're going. Patience, old friend." Then she caressed his sagging back. The little Beagle rubbed his head against her pants leg and shook the tags on his collar as if to hurry her along, too. "We'll get there, Barney."

I glanced at my cell phone. "I have to go. Margaret. I have a conference call at 1:30 so I better let you get back to your walk." We went our ways.

That night I got the call that Margaret had met her own appointment with Death. A mutual friend had found her. Our friend, Julie, told me what she saw. "Margaret had collapsed sitting with her "sweet ones" as they sat in the backyard. The dogs had also died with her. All three dogs had been lying around her, touching her as they all made the last journey."

I rushed to Margaret's to help Julie. As I made the short walk I kept thinking there was something here that I was missing. Margaret had more than three dogs with her when I'd seen her that afternoon. Where were the other dogs? What had happened to the dogs who died with her?

Julie opened the door for me as I walked up to the lighted door. She had been crying. "Thank you for coming. Margaret and the dogs are out back. I didn't want to move them until the ambulance got here."

Julie and I walked out to where Margaret lay with her last old dogs around her. The paramedics had walked in right before me and the two women were busy checking Margaret's body. There was the Shih Tzu I had seen. He was cuddled up against her chest under her right arm. The Beagle, Barney, lay on her other side with his head over her waist as if he was just sleeping. There was a pit bull girl here, too. I'd seen her in today's walk but had not heard her name. But where were the other dogs? Where was Max the Lab? Had he gotten loose? Were there old dogs wandering lost around the neighborhood?

"Julie, are there any other dogs here?"

"No. These are the only dogs Margaret had."

"Are you sure? I saw her earlier today and there were at least ten dogs with her."

One of the paramedics, a middle-aged Black woman, stood up from Margaret's body and walked over to me. "Ma'am, when did you see the deceased?"

I thought for a minute and pulled my reading glasses off my head where I had parked them. "It must have been about 1 PM because I was walking back from lunch over at the grill a few blocks over."

The paramedic looked away at Margaret's body and then back at me. "Are you really sure about that?"

"No doubt. But she had more dogs with her when I saw her. Where are they?

Julie put a soft hand on my left arm. "No, Margaret only had these three dogs now. The odd thing is these three dogs just seem to have vied. None of them were in really bad health. It's as if they just decided to go with her."

I turned and walked back into Margaret's all-too quiet house. Julie came in behind me but I wasn't listening to her right then. I must have been looking for something, anything to help me understand what happened to the other dogs.

The paramedic came in behind me and put her hand on my right shoulder. "I hate to ask you again when you saw your friend today but bear with me. Are you absolutely sure you saw her walking dogs at 1 PM?"

I turned toward her concerned face. "Absolutely. Why are you so interested in the last time I saw Margaret?"

The woman glanced at Julie and back to me. She ran her hand through her short hair and tugged at a small gold hoop earring. "Well, ma'am, I'm not doubting you but your friend passed early this morning. According to what we see the latest she could have passed would be around 10 AM. There's no way she could have been walking dogs at 1."

I lost my breath and took a few steps back, coming to lean against the bookshelf hosting the dog photos. Julie reached out to me to keep me from falling. I turned to avoid the two women's doubtful glances. As I did, I realized where I had seen Max before. Max, complete with white muzzle stared out at me from a photo and gold embossed frame that very clearly proclaimed, "Max— passed 2007."

Then I knew where the other dogs were and who they were. Margaret's "sweet ones" had not forgotten her.

She had seen them through Death's gate and they had returned to make sure she was not alone on her journey. They had taken the last walk with her.

Life often catches all of us by surprise but in this sweet story by Sandra Murphy one dog helps his Mama find a brighter life.

Denali

by Sandra Murphy

Peg was blindsided by a cliché named Steffi-with-an-i, a sized zero, twenty-two year old former cheerleader and newly hired receptionist at John's company. Peg hadn't been a size two since, well, never. When she was twenty-two, the only size two was a 2T, as in T for toddler. Looking at it from the dark side of forty, Peg thought 2T was a perfect fit for someone who dotted an i with a little smiley face.

Nighttime noises, creaks and groans, comforting and familiar when John was there, became a reason to lose sleep after he left. With dark circles beneath her eyes, crow's feet growing into ruts and her appetite a distant memory, Peg consulted her doctor. An old-fashioned sort, he reached for the prescription pad, wrote a few words and handed the slip to Peg. "You don't see it yet but this is a beginning, not an end." He patted her hand, the one that used to wear a gold band. "This will fix you up. Fill it right away."

Peg stuffed the paper into her old shoulder bag before she embarrassed herself by crying, paid the nurse and headed to her old car. Once she was behind the wheel and safely belted in, she looked to see what miracle drug the doctor had prescribed. Four carefully printed words read, "Get a big dog." Peg laughed for the first time in weeks. She gave herself a good look in the rearview mirror, decided it was time for some long overdue changes and drove straight to the adoption center where she found Denali.

Denali was a big brown dog of indeterminate parentage. His ears flopped, his tail went more left than not, and he smiled, a big, slobbery, toothy grin. His enthusiasm for life could have caused problems for Peg—John's favorite chair fell victim to Denali's curiosity about what caused it to squeak. Peg told Denali, "Good dog! John doesn't need that chair anyway. Steffi-with-an-i never gives him time to sit down." Denali smiled.

On the other side of town, Art came home from his business trip to find a note from Sue, stuck to the fridge with a magnet advertising a local divorce lawyer. It wasn't as short as the doctor's note to Peg but it came close. "I'm leaving you to find myself. Don't call."

It seemed that for Sue to find herself, she needed every piece of the Ikea furniture she'd picked out, the cash from their checking account and her yoga instructor, Ramesh Boyd.

Art's doctor told him to get out more, like he had anything to sit on at home. "Get out and do what?" Art asked. Art had worked so much, he had no idea what people did with spare time.

"You'll know it when you see it," his doctor replied. "Do something unexpected."

Art went to the park to read the paper and drink his coffee before work each day. He felt silly, a grown man, sitting there in a suit and tie, surrounded by nannies and their charges, waiting for something to happen, something unexpected, something to make getting out, or even getting up, worthwhile. For two weeks, there was nothing except fresh air, pigeons that begged and squirrels that chattered gibberish.

Then he met Denali.

During a run in the park, Denali pulled his leather leash from Peg's hand and took off at a gallop, only to jump on a not-quite-handsome, age appropriate man reading a newspaper. Peg was afraid to look but peeked from squinted eyes. The business section was in shreds and Denali was getting his first taste of coffee with cream from Art's blue tie—but Art was laughing.

Things went well between Peg and Art. They were careful with each other's feelings and took their time getting to know one another. They played tennis if you could call it that—he served, she returned. Her serves never got across the net; his returns were always out of bounds. The farmer's market became a frequent stop for new foods to try. Resale shops supplied new-to-him furniture for Art, painted in colors not seen in nature, just for the fun of it.

Then one day, John showed up at Peg's door. Steffi-with-an-i had lost patience with him, "A man as old as my Dad" she'd said, "who can't even go out clubbing during the week."

John's timing couldn't have been worse—Art showed up for dinner to find John holding Peg's hand, asking for a second chance and assuming the answer would be yes, of course. Art's face went through a variety of emotions before settling on a blank mask.

John had no doubt that Peg would take him back. Even if he couldn't go clubbing every night, he was a catch—

hadn't he just been living with a twenty-two year old girlfriend? His mind erased her remark about his age. "Thanks, umm, Art, I appreciate you spending time with Peg while I was, umm, away. Now that I'm back, you can get on with your own life." Turning to Peg, he said, "Is that spaghetti sauce I smell? You know it upsets my stomach. Do you think you could get some meat, maybe a roast, and baked potatoes ready by the time I get back? There's a good girl." He missed the look in Peg's eyes. "You can get my chair out of the spare room too. There's a game on tonight."

Before Peg could speak, Denali ran to John, red rubber ball in his mouth. "What's he want?" John asked. "Hey, Art, you got a fenced yard? Maybe you could take the dog. Peg won't need him now that I'm back."

Peg smiled. "He wants to play ball—but not in the house. Why don't you head outside while I talk to Art? You go out the door first—it's an Alpha Dog thing."

"Oh sure, you want to say goodbye, I can understand that. Take your time. I've got a few minutes." John opened the front door and stepped out onto the porch. Denali jumped up, put his big paws on the door and slammed it shut before John could turn around.

"That's the best trick you ever taught him," Art said as he took Peg into his arms. "I thought John was going to stay forever."

"No way," said Peg. "The question is, will you?"

Denali smiled.

For Love of Steam is our only steam punk entry in this anthology. It first appeared in the anthology Dreams of steam *(Kerlak Publishing) where it was a finalist for the Darrell Award.,This love story is told from a surprising yet knowledgeable viewpoint.*

For the Love of Steam

by Missa Dixon

Life changed for us after Daddy left. Mama worked tirelessly, day and night, in her workshop. We never went for walks anymore and, although I love Mrs. Baxter, our housekeeper, she never gave treats like mama did. Now-a-days Mama would wake before dawn, wash, pull on her petticoats and dress as she ran down the stairs to her shop, picking up the welding goggles she had left hanging on the end of the banister the night before. I would get a soft pat on the head as her skirt brushed by me in the doorway. Off she would go, lost in her dark world. I would take my place on the well-worn rug she lovingly placed under her workbench. Many hours would pass and then, well after the light was gone from the windows, Mama would drag herself up the stairs pulling off her goggles and leaving them on the banister, for another day's toil was now done; a scene to be replayed before the sunlight in the windows returned.

One day the great steam bell interrupted our daily routine. Mama had replaced the normal door knocker like all the other houses had with a much higher-power noise maker, one so loud she would hear it ring in her workshop, even on

Mrs. Baxter's day off. Like I wasn't a good enough doorbell - I would bark at the milkman who came every day. Of course, I could hear a stranger come up the stoop and tell her about it. But I don't think she understands my dog barking.

Once again the steam roared through the house. I leaped off my warm rug and rushed to the door, barking all the while.

"Damn it!" Mama cursed, "Mrs. Baxter, please get the door!" She yelled.

Walking up behind me, Mama said, "Is it her day off, Charlie? I didn't think it was Thursday already."

The great bell rang again. "Coming!" Mama yelled at the door.

Grabbing the handle firmly, Mama flung open the large, heavy door that thudded as it came to an abrupt stop against the adjacent wall.

"May I help you?" She angrily challenged the man standing in front of her. She had not even removed her goggles, much less her welding apron. To any stranger Mama probably looked frightful, but I loved her with all my heart and I was not going to let anyone hurt her. I was a good guard dog and I also looked sternly at the man standing on my veranda.

The man now standing on the oversized front porch was dress in long, dark pants and a matching shorter frock coat that had become the popular style for upper-class dandies. A light colored shirt and dark bow tie finished his clothing. His dark, worn, leather topcoat was laid over his left arm with his rain stained top hat held in his left hand. He had obviously just dashed through the downpour from the waiting carriage, parked on the street in front of our house. A puff of steam jettisoned out the back just as he began to speak.

"I'm looking for Miss Stephanie Tapp of 92 Cotton Street." He said in a light, cheery, yet somehow annoyed voice.

"I am she. How can I help you?" Mama answered flatly.

"I'm Drake Maloney from the Philadelphia Science Conservatory." He held up a rolled up addition of *Scientific American* magazine, showing the rag to Mama. "And we've heard of you and your work."

"Anyone can pick up a science journal and any educated man can read it. So once again I ask, how can I help you?" Mama said roughly as she pulled her goggles down off her piercing green eyes. They matched her dress even down to the small golden stripes running down her skirt. Her petticoats were stained gray from years in workshops but the apron she wore showed off the warm, silky brown of her long hair nicely. She didn't like to go shopping for anything. She prefrred to scrounge up useful items and bring them back to life.

Mrs. Baxter, the housekeeper, did everything to keep the house running, but she drew the line at Mama's personal shopping. The newest thing Mama had on was her welding apron; it was the last thing Daddy had bought for her before he had gone away. Most women would have been horrified at such a gift. But I think Mama liked it better than the ring he had given her when we all went up in the air-ship for the Halloween Ball, now three cold seasons ago. Mama said we became a family that night and that Daddy was now my Daddy and she was still my Mommy, and we would live together forever. Funny how things changed for us.

The man's voice jostled me from my daydream. I had to make sure Mama was safe from this stranger. I stared him down and growled in a low voice just so he would remember that I was there ready to strike if he came closer to us.

"You've heard the World's Fair is coming to America, Philadelphia to be exact. The whole globe is coming to celebrate one hundred years of freedom in our great land." He said with a slight southern accent.

Curious how a man from the south talked about great things happening in a thriving northern city, just ten years after *The War Against Northern Aggression,* this was Memphis, Tennessee after all. I could tell Mama was intrigued. Plus he had a steam coach. Mama had never seen one before - at least not one so big.

"Yes Mr. Maloney the Centennial International Exhibition will open in your fair city in just over a year – July 4th, 1876 I believe. What has that got to do with me and my work?" My mother repeated a bit warmer than before. I could tell she wanted to know more about what this man had to offer. Maybe even have a ride in his carriage.

A wide smile came across the man's face. "You are working on little steam, Miss Tapp. You're creating the world's smallest steam engines has excited the curiosity of the selection committee and we would like you to show off your work on the world's biggest stage."

"It's Dr. Tapp to you sir, and it's called Micro Steam, Mr. Maloney." Mama corrected him. "And I have no interest in being gawked at as a freak by strangers who will have no appreciation for the glory of technology."

A confused look came over the man's face as Mama slammed the big door on the man with a huff. She turned to find Mrs. Baxter standing behind her having just returned from her errands.

Mrs. Baxter had been Mama's housekeeper since before I came to live with Mama just as the rebels from both sides of the war began their assault on the west – three years after the Great War. Mama found me in the rubble of a warehouse that had been bombed during the last battle on the Mississippi River. She had been looking for scrap metal to continue her work. But instead she found a small white puppy with brown spots. I guess she felt sorry for me and took me home. Mrs. Baxter was there when we walked in, and she appeared to have everything in hand.

I remember Mama explaining to her what had happened. "I was in the bombed cotton warehouse on Front Street, looking through the bits and pieces for anything useful. I found a dead dog under one of the collapsed walls. Kind of unsettling if you ask me. Then I heard a noise. Thinking it might be something useful - gears, steel rods - just anything. I moved some bricks and out toppled this ball of fur."

"I see, my lady." Always very proper was Mrs. Baxter.

"I couldn't leave him there. Plus this place could use some livening up." Mama continued with a happy giggle she no longer had.

Mrs. Baxter, looking very put out if memory serves, "He's going to make a mess. But your father left you the house and you may do, as you will with it. But I will not be his caretaker."

"What shall I yell at the dog when he misbehaves?" Mrs. Baxter asked flatly.

Mama looked puzzled at her for a moment. "Oh yes, a name!" Mama thought and thought, as Mrs. Baxter put down a warm bowl of soup she had just finished. I remember it was the best thing I ever ate.

"Who was that Englishman who won the Coplay Medal several years ago?" Mama pondered. "You know, the survival of the fittest gentleman."

"I most certainly do not." Mrs. Baxter chimed back as she refilled the small bowl on the floor with another ladle of broth.

"Charles. Yes Charles Darwin. We'll call him Charlie." Mama said happily.

I digress into the past but Mrs. Baxter's voice brought me back to the here and now. "Bad things happen. Your precious Ben died; however, for you, life has gone on. Your father left you with the knowledge and the skills to build yourself up again and carry on disfigured as you think you are." Mrs. Baxter pointed at my mama's left leg - the one that went away with Daddy and she replaced with a brass one. "And even though you hide all day in the dark of your workroom, the sun rose, just as it will rise again tomorrow morning. "Charles Darwin Dog Tapp needs to be walked by his mistress." She has always referred to me by my full name.

"You need to talk to real people, not the life size dolls you work on every day. You made yourself walk again. Now show the world that they can walk again as well." She turned in a whirl of her black dress, back toward the kitchen. I almost followed her. She always brought me something back from the butcher and the warm memories of happier times called to me. But

Mama needed me now. So I stayed at her heels just in case a warm dog kiss was needed to salve old wounds.

With a heavy look, a tear dropped from Mama's eye. Then she inhaled more deeply that I had ever seen her do. She grabbed the door and slowly it began to move. "Mr. Maloney!" Mama's voice called out the now open door. "Tell your people I will be there. But I have some conditions."

"Ask for just about anything and I can deliver it you, Miss…" He stopped himself, "Sorry Dr. Tapp."

"I will require medium-sized booth in the Main Exhibition Building at the World's Fair. Also, we will need four-star room and board for myself, Mrs. Baxter, Charles and our guest." Mama instructed.

"Done." Mr. Maloney answered, revealing more of his Southern ways.

"Don't be so hasty. I'm not done yet, sir. You will pay for all money expenses including travel expenses for us all. A weekly stipend for Mrs. Baxter and our guest in the amount of $5.00 starting now till the fair is over." her voice trailed off.

"That is all very reasonable." He replied with a hint of excitement in his voice. "Anything else?"

"Yes. Our guest. I need a wounded man, a veteran from the war, preferably. One that lost one or both legs and is young enough, strong enough, and willing to walk again. Can you find me such a man?" Mama finished.

"Oh yes, Dr. Tapp. I know the perfect man. He will be here, where I stand, in one month." Mr. Maloney then dashed down the stairs into the rain and swung open his taxi's door. "You are going to be famous, Dr. Tapp. You just wait and see."

"We shall see." Mama quietly replied as she closed the door.

She wandered into the kitchen with me at her heels. "Mrs. Baxter, would you make up the spare room? We will be having a guest."

"Of course, my lady." She said with that proper smile.

For the first time since Daddy left, Mama pulled off her goggles and ascended the stairs before the light left the sky. I did not follow. I knew she was going to sleep and cry and she would not want me with her in the dark cloud of grief.

*****

In the morning, Mama rose after dawn. She began to refit the house with the steam lifts and other devices that she had used after Daddy had gone. Piping that Mama had taken down after she could walk again was relayed. The chairs that connected to the banisters that lifted Mama to her bedroom and from the front stoop were reconnected and tested. She hired a dustman, Mr. Gage, to help her with the lifting and cleaning up the outside of the house. She wanted everything to look good for the new tenant.

I could tell Mama's heart was still sad but it seemed there was light in her eyes once again. Mrs. Baxter even said so to Mrs. Trudy Worthington, the next-door housekeeper, when she took me for my walk. "Thank the stars, Trudy. Dr. Tapp appears to have finally turned a corner. She ate a full meal yesterday. And she asked the dustman to clear the back patio of over-growth." Her excitement evident in her retelling of the tale. "For these last few years, since Ben

111

was killed, I didn't think she was going to come back, even after she built that leg of hers."

Mama had asked Mrs. Baxter to tidy up the house, in hopes of making it more presentable to their guest. Mrs. Baxter hired a girl to help clean out the three years of gloom. Everything that was not nailed down was washed, scrubbed, pressed, polished, shined, remade, re-hung, mended, or thrown out. New white wash was put on the walls, and new paper was hung in all the public formal areas. Of course, Mama worked in her workshop but she spent time "outing the old and ining the new." At least that what she kept saying. I was even taken to the groomer and bathed and clipped to within an inch of my life. The month had been a true whirlwind. However, the house looked amazing – like somebody lived here – not a dark mausoleum ready for the not-yet-dead. On the last day, Mama even gave me a new collar and leash. We went walking down the street to the park just to try it out. We had not done that in three cold seasons. Life was looking up for my little family.

*****

In the hubbub of the past month I had almost forgotten our guest. As promised, one month later the great bell rung again. Mama rushed past everyone to open it. She was expecting a grizzled, broken, old man, supporting himself on makeshift crutches and wooden legs. However, the universe had a different idea. A young street urchin stood on her porch.

"Dr. Tapp?" he said in a very southern accent.

"Yes, I'm Dr. Tapp." Mama answered coarsely. She didn't like the street trash. Schools were what these children needed. Let knowledge set them free from their earthly bonds. I growled at the kid, just to make sure he knew Mama meant business and this was no place to play.

He backed up, turned around and ran down the stairs saying, "This is the place Mister. I want my two cents now. And you didn't say nothing about a dog."

Mama's eyes followed the child down her steps to the street and what appeared to be the same carriage that had brought Mr. Maloney. It now opened up like a great steam organ and a man appeared sitting in a wheeled chair. The chair was not that different from the one she had made for herself after Ben had been killed and she had lost her leg.

The carriage lowered and the man rolled himself off the lift and onto the walk in front of the stairs with great ease. The man, covered by a duster-style coat and a large hat, tossed two shinny coins to the boy. "Thanks kid! Now get on - Dr. Tapp doesn't appear to like youngsters youngin's."

He looked around; surveying the area, then asked gently, "May I use your lift?" His voice was southern but refined and educated.

"Oh yes. I re-erected it for your use." Mama paused. "I'm surprised you know what it is." A smile could be heard in her voice and she could not hide the surprised look on her face by the fact this gentleman knew what her lift was.

"I've seen your designs before - clever to say the least." He commented.

The veteran pulled himself into the waiting chair, reached under the seat, and started the lift. Mama's jaw dropped as the steam rose from the metal banisters and the chair began to rise. Because of the use of his chair his arms were enormous with muscle. So it was with no great surprise he used one of his great arms he to picked up his wheeled chair and let the lift carry him and his chair to the top of the stoop. I could see it in her eyes. *Who is this? And how does he know how to use my lift?*

I barked once to bring her back. We were going to be face to face with this man in a minute and Mama needed to be on her toes.

The gentleman placed his chair down on the porch with one graceful motion. Then as if he had done this a thousand times before he transferred himself from the lift to his old chair. A massive, light colored hat had been obscuring his features.

However, now that he had arrived here on the stoop, the man removed it and introduced himself. "Dr. Tapp, my name is Vincent Malone. I am your experiment for the next year."

Mama and Mrs. Baxter, who had now joined us on the porch, were speechless. The war had been over for almost ten years – depending on how you asked. And the *War in the West* had been quiet for almost two years. However, this man was young – no more than mid-thirties - Mama's age. How could he have fought in the war yet kept his vigor? I know Mama was expecting an old, broken man. I had heard her say many times to Mr. Gage, "My biggest challenge will not the making of the devices but convincing the geezer to use them and get his broken soul to live again."

Mrs. Baxter had also been dubious about an old veteran coming to stay. "He'd better keep his hands to himself." She would explain. "I will put him in his place if he tries anything. I've got knives, and I know how to use them." Mrs. Baxter might have been old but she was a spry lady when it came to her person.

Mrs. Trudy Worthington would smile back, "If he's that much of a ruffian send him to me. Let him chase me around in that wheeled contraption."

It appeared no one had to worry. Mr. Malone was strong, willing, a true gentleman, and very handsome to boot. Long dark wavy brown hair with just the first hints of gray covered his head. Bright, clear, shinning green eyes twinkled over a well-groomed beard. His slightly western style clothing looked like it was made for him exactly. The coat he wore covered his massive arms without straining. His shirt buttoned perfectly over his expansive chest. Even his pants ended in neat hems right above what would have been his knees.

"Not what you were expecting, I see." He broke the silence.

"I apologize ,Sir. I meant no disrespect by staring, of course. I know for a fact that the pressure of all those eyes can be infuriating. However, I," she stuttered, "I mean we, were expecting a much different kind of man." My mother answered.

A warm smile came over Mr. Malone's face. "I think my brother did good getting us together. And what needs to get done first?"

"Your brother, sir?" Mama asked with a puzzled look on her face.

"My brother Drake, he's the one that came to you a month ago and asked for your help." He answered in a matter a fact way.

"I see." Mama mumbled.

"I still need your Micro-Steam, and so do lots of other people, Dr. Tapp. So let's get started. Introductions and then where do I bunk down?"

Mama held her ground for a minute, and then as if something had lifted, she started the introductions. "Oh yes, well I'm Dr. Stephanie Tapp. Please call me Dr. Tapp. This is Mrs. Baxter, my housekeeper." Mr. Malone nodded in recognition.

"Here is your payment, Mrs. Baxter." Handing her a dark brown leather envelope, "My brother told me that we had agreed to five dollars a week. This is that payment in full money for my room and board. That should cover it. I put some extra in just in case I eat a lot." He said with a bright laughing smile. Mama and Mrs. Baxter were so stunned by his gesture that I had been left out of the introductions. I had to bark to remind her to tell him about me.

"Oh yes this is Charles Darwin. You can call him Charlie. He's our center in this house." She explained to this new human.

He put his hand down for me to smell. I obliged him. I could tell he had been around all kinds of animals and that he understood basic hygiene. Also, he might have no had legs but that had not stopped him from working with his hands or firing guns.

The rest of the day was spent showing our guest around and loading his things into his quarters. He could already use Mama's helping machines, so the time teaching him how to get around was saved. Mr. Malone explained that he and his brother had seen her ideas in print. Tinkering with those plans, the brothers had made their childhood home more accessible. Vincent also let it be known that he had made some improvements on Mama's designs so that he could be lifted onto a horse without scaring the beast to death. I could tell Mama was warming up to this veteran. She was too fascinated by his conversation and at dinner she forgot to give me my part of her steak under the table as she always did.

"Yes, Dr. Tapp, I have done everything to make my world fit this body I was left with. However, walking again would bring me to the best part of my life. When I got my copy of that rag last year and saw your steam limb, I just had to get a hold of you." He stated brightly, "What happened that you lost your leg?"

Mama's heart fell. I could see it like a shroud that had been wrapped around her lifted for a short time, but now, with this innocent question, it closed up around her again. I put my paw on top of hers and looked up into her shaking green eyes. I wanted her to feel my love. However, Mama finally answered, "The War. *The War in the West* took the whole of my life." Then she rose from the dinner table and trudged up the stairs – leaving behind her momentary retreat from the pain of her loss.

Mrs. Baxter placed her hand on Mr. Malone's hand. "She will give you new legs. And I hope to all the Gods above you give her a new heart."

"What happened?" Mr. Malone asked.

"Very simple actually. Do you remember a few years ago when the rebels reformed and started attacking outposts up and down the river?" Mrs. Baxter asked.

"Oh yes." Mr. Malone answered. "I couldn't get my livestock to market and I couldn't get supplies in for over a year because of all the trouble."

"Well," Mrs. Baxter continued as she pulled a bit of Yorkshire pudding off the hunk and gave half of it to me. "Dr. Tapp and her beloved Benjamin Watt had met at a symposium held at the new Arboretum. They were both attending a talk about steam or some such. They were like two peas in a pod - both so into the newest technology. I've never seen two people so in love in all my life. Their – light – was infectious."

"However," Mrs. Baxter continued, "the war flared up again along this Big Old River, especially here in Memphis. And it was not long before Ben, who was an engineer on the river, was pressed into service keeping the river open for barge and boat traffic. It didn't matter to them – Ben and the Mrs. they refused the glum pawl over the area and gleefully pressed forward with their weeding plans."

"One night late Ben had brought home new welding vests for Stephanie and himself to celebrate her first publication. They were to be married at the next full moon. Ben joked about wearing their new matching vest as part of their wedding attire. Then a knock at the door - a young man had been sent to collect Ben. Someone had destroyed part of a levee that kept the river back. Men who could build with metal were needed. So Ben had to go or part of the Low City would be flooded by morning. Stephanie went with him to help. She had just finished her welding course. There were only a few people who could weld in those days. The River Master was happy for her help."

"They worked all night holding the water back. Charlie and I made a huge breakfast for their return." She patted me on the head and gave me the other half of the pudding. "But they never did."

"What happened to them?" Mr. Malone asked.

"As the sun rose there was another attack. I was told it was the biggest explosion since the war. Ben was killed instantly and Miss Stephanie…" She paused as if a bayonet had stabbed her own heart. She had lost her left leg. It was blown off as she was trying to weld the last piece of metal in place."

"I finally found her two days later in the hospital. She was still unconscious but the doctors had already taken her leg off, repaired the wound, and stabilized her blood loss. They were hopeful she would live but they knew she would never walk again." Mrs. Baxter continued.

"I moved into the hospital - caring for her day and night. Charlie became the hospital mascot - running each and every floor, visiting with everyone just to cheer him or her up. I still take him there every week to help out the sick and injured. After three months, they let me take her home. She had not spoken to anyone. The doctors were afraid that she needed to go to a sanitarium for further treatment. I knew I needed to get her home for her to heal."

"As soon as we got to the steps, she flew into action. She had built a wheeled chair in less than a day, and a steam one in about a fortnight. The house had lifts throughout a month after that and she strapped on her first leg in less than half a year. So much for what doctors know!" Mrs. Baxter sneered.

"She could walk but her spirit was as cold as a January morning. Work, write, and cry that's all she has done lo these many years. Her flame has burned far and wide but nothing has warmed her since that night so long ago." Now finished with her story Mrs. Baxter wiped away a tear.

"I didn't know she had lost a leg. I just saw the brilliance of her work and hoped she could help me live just a little better in a world not made for men who have fallen from the grace of perfections." Vincent countered.

"I will see myself to bed. Thanks for letting me know what I'm in for." He rolled away and the great steam lift could be heard churning him up the stairs.

Mrs. Baxter cleaned the table, set up the starter for the bread and went to bed soon after. I went to my Mama's room and slept outside her door just in case she needed me to lick away the tears.

*****

As usual, Mama was up, washed, dressed and at her post before the sun rose. Our guest was waiting for her with that wide, bright smile and welding clothes of his own. I could tell Mama was put off and intrigued at the same time. They went straight to work. With the extra money now in the house, Mrs. Baxter had made a fine breakfast so everyone could get started off on the right foot. I was the only one to partake of her labors. She complained bitterly about our lack of respect for her work and trouble. She even went so far as to threaten to not make lunch or dinner. However, there were sandwiches on the table at the noon hour and braised pork chops in gravy for dinner.

All day Mama and Mr. Malone worked on his legs. Measuring, weighing, planning, and arguing. It was like a never-ending science talk and a high stakes poker game all wrapped up into one. Mama would say something. Malone would counter. Round and round they went. By the end of the day they ate in different rooms and yelled back and forth to each other about not wanting to talk because the other one had no intelligence. I was happy for the start of the process. I got twice the dinner; one from Mama and one from Mr. Malone. Yummmy.

As the weeks wore on progress seemed to be slow. More arguing, more planning, more ideas to improve Mama's overall design ruled each day. The one thing Mrs. Baxter noticed was that the personal-ness of their first attacks at each other was gone. They were more playful, even throwing her corn muffins at each other one night.

"They made a mess of my dining room last night!" Mrs. Baxter explained to Mrs. Worthington while they were out on a walk. "I have not seen such juvenile behavior since I was in Sunday school."

Mrs. Worthington smiled widely, revealing her missing teeth, "Well the lovers' moon might just rise over the Tapp house again. About time don't you think?"

Mrs. Baxter's voice cracked as she answered, "Oh yes! Oh yes my dear. We can hope."

*****

Mr. Malone had been with us for over half a year. Mrs. Baxter had put heavy restriction on how much they could feed me. It appears I was getting too fat to walk the park with her in the mornings at her normal pace. I couldn't help the fact that I was cute and they loved to feed me. However, Mama and Mr. Malone had started taking me out in the evening after dinner to scavenge for materials. They didn't do any real scavenging but it was how they got to know one another and settled the day's differences so no one went to bed mad.

"So Mrs. Baxter spilled the beans about me. Well fair is fair. How did you lose your legs?" Mama asked one day as we rounded the park.

Mr. Malone smiled, "I was wondering when you were going to ask."

"I was just waiting till we had the time." Mama responded warmly.

She found a bench and sat down. I hopped up next to her and put my paws in her lap. Spring had come but the evenings were still chilled and I liked my paws warm. Mr. Malone guided the great steam chair next to us, so close he could hold Mama's hand, if things got to scary for her.

"We live on the west side of this great river." He pointed at the mighty Mississippi flowing down below the bluffs. "My family owns a huge ranch not a day's ride west from here. When the war broke out, my father felt it was not our business to get involved. He kept me and my bother home to run the ranch and protect our interest from both sides."

Although Mama never approved of war in the first place, finding me in that building had helped turn her mind against the idea of war as a way to settle conflicts. With her head against the idea, her heart was turned with the death of Daddy. So she approved of Vincent's father's neutral stance as the lunacy raged around them. "Your father was a brave man in those days." She added.

"Both sides did bad things west of the river, neither one-made friends. For many of us Westies, neutrality was the only way to keep your land and your life." He added.

"After Lee signed to Grant, the war in the west took off. In the winter of sixty-six, troops came to the ranch and asked for ten head of cattle to feed themselves over the winter holiday. My father told them to see me - I was the quartermaster in those days - and pay for them. They could have their pick, but only after they paid. They hunted me down in my bunkhouse and told me to give them ten head. I didn't know what they were talking about but I told them it would cost them 100 gold dollars if they wanted the cattle. I guess they didn't like my answer because one of the soldiers hit me from behind with the butt of his gun. I fought back of course. Killed two of them but I just couldn't get them all. One of them clocked me in the back of the head. They took my keys to the steer pin and started shooting the cattle."

"My Dad had an idea something might happen. He mobilized the men we had on hand at the ranch. The solders must have been with a platoon that had artillery, because before my Father's men could take up their post, cannon fire rang out on the ranch. I was coming around after being pistol whipped, when the bunkhouse exploded around me. All I remember is being thrown to the ground. I woke up in the main house with doctors all around me. My brother and the rest of the ranch hands had finally driven the solders off, but my Dad had been killed in the fight and I had lost both of my legs."

"You must have been upset when you woke up. I know I was so angry and hurt I just couldn't move." Mama said.

"I was pissed that my Father had been killed for ten cattle but I never gave up. I never let my sadness or hurt take me. My brother was much more the city man than me and he heard about this new steam technology and the wonders it might do. I started working with these great new engines. I made some really helpful improvements to others' inventions. I even helped make sheep and cattle herding easier with a steam-powered cart. I used one of Rumford's ideas and improved the oven in the house. And I even found you and the idea that I could get new steam legs to walk on so that no one would be the wiser." He reached out to touch Mama's hand that had been petting me. "I just didn't know the person who had invented the idea of Micro-Steam was such a beautiful, smart, talented woman."

Mama blushed and looked away towards the river with an embarrassed smile on her face. I could feel the warmth rising in her body. Mr. Malone raised his hand from Mama's to her face. Gently, he moved her head so they were starring into each other's eyes. He leaned close to her and she leaned into him almost, smushing me in between. Their lips met in a warm, wet exhale. I took the opportunity to lick two faces at once.

"Charlie!" Mama exclaimed. "What are you doing?"

While Mama was distracted, Vincent scooped both of us up with his superhuman arms and placed us on his lap. He encircled Mama, making sure I was outside his arms, and kissed her deeply. Mama melted into his embrace.

"No woman has ever stolen my heart, Dr. Stephanie Tapp." Vincent removed a gold clockwork heart from a chain around his neck. "Here it is. All for you." He said softly.

Mama lit up like one of her torches. She took the charm and slid it into her bustier near her heart. She re-adjusted herself on Vincent's lap, kissing him again, and saying, "Home sir, we have legs to build."

I hopped off her lap and ran behind the steam chair as they raced home. I wondered if he was going to be my new Daddy. Mama had not said anything yet, but she sure acted like it.

*****

The next morning, boxes of all kinds arrived on the front stoop. Most said Tiffany &Co. The rest were just the normal plate brass by the smell of them. Mama and Vincent loaded the boxes into the workshop and didn't leave for four days. The heavy sound of metal work could be heard day and night. Welding of tiny pipes, gears, jewelers' chains took over from the talking and arguing that ruled the first days of their working relationship. Heated discussions could still be heard from time to time emanating from the workshop but from the most part – work, work, work.

Mrs. Baxter took food at regular intervals and sometimes I heard her scream, "Don't sleep on the tables. It's unseemly. What will the neighbors think? At least pretend to go to bed once a day."

When the light was waning from the windows on the fourth day, Vincent walked from the workshop. Looking like he had not bathed in a week, with welding soot all over his face and shirt, he walked from the workshop with two new legs under him. Mrs. Baxter just about dropped the dinner tray she was carrying into the workshop. Mama came up behind him, and she looked even worse that he did. Her long brown hair was now almost black, and her once green dress was now a dull gray from welding ash. But her face glowed. Pride. Happiness. Relief. Joy. And maybe even a hint of love showed all over her person.

"I can't believe it, Sir. You are standing in this entryway. Tall and strong as any man alive," Mrs. Baxter uttered.

"Yes distinguished lady. I stand. But I would not be the man I am without having lost my legs. I would not have found my love." Vincent turned to Mama, and kneeling down took her hand and said, "Will you marry me, Dr. Tapp."

Mama was aghast. I was aghast. She was a woman true, but she was missing her left leg and how could any man want her - even one that was missing both of his legs. She was damaged goods, as she would often say.

Seeing her mind churning, Vincent clutched her lovingly and exclaimed as if to the world, "I want you even with one leg. Will you have me with none?"

"Yes!" She said through tears coming up in her eyes. "Yes! YES!" Mama continued as Vincent picked her up and whirled her around.

When he put Mama down, she picked me up and said, "Charlie, you have a new Daddy. Aren't you happy?"

Like I didn't know that was coming. I licked her face and wagged my tail as much as I could without my feet on the ground. I could tell Mama was overjoyed. Mrs. Baxter was in tears, leaning against the wall giving thanks to everything she could for the positive turn of events. My new Daddy was smiling like I had never seen a man smile before.

From out of nowhere, drinks appeared, and everyone did a shot and threw the small glasses into the fire. Then off to bed, for there was much to do when the sun rose and only half a year to the expo in the far off place called Philadelphia.

*****

Mama and my new Daddy did not waste any time. They were married at the downtown courthouse the next week. I had to wait outside with the rings tied to my new collar because they had changed the laws. "No Dogs Allowed While Court is in Session" was what the sign said, and getting married was the court being in session. They came out of the courthouse and right down to the riverboat for a month-long honeymoon.

I don't think I'd ever seen Mama so happy. During this time Daddy completely mastered his legs; taking them off, putting them on, and filling them with pure water and tiny stones that kept the steam going. Their days were filled with talk and walks on the decks taking in all the sights of the mighty Mississippi River.

When the two of them returned they started building the exhibit they would take to the World's Fair. Micro-Steam was going to be all the rage. Once again the house hummed with excitement. But this time no cloud of sad darkness rested over the large Victorian style home in the middle of Cotton Street. Plumes of steam, the sounds of industry, and always the smell of roasting beef had replaced the darkness. After all, Daddy was a cattleman from right across the river. Fresh meat got delivered to the house every week and I couldn't have been happier.

*****

Spring was now waning into summer as a new set of three new steam wagons pulled up to the house. Mr. Gage, who had been working on the exterior of the house repairing and painting almost, fell off his ladder because of surprise. The opening of the World's Fair was only ten weeks away and all submissions must be checked in and operating by June 4th.

"They're amazing, Vincent! Where did you get them? How did you get them built? Will they make it all the way to Philadelphia?" Mama asked emphatically.

"I've been having them built at the ranch. I figure we can get to Philly in half the time using steam, even over some of those bad roads crossing the Smoky Mountains." Daddy replied wearing this trademark wide smile framed by his long dark hair and beard. "These are some of the hands that will be helping us load everything and carrying it for us."

One of the men stepped forward, his face obscured by his wide brimmed brown hat. As he looked up, Stephanie recognized him as Drake Maloney the young man that had brought her this new life. "Dr. Tapp," he removed his hat and lowered his eyes in respect. "I can't thank you enough for bring my brother back. It would be my pleasure to take your equipment to show the world a whole life can be lived no matter if the body is whole or not. Everything is paid for and ready to go."

"Well, well, Mr. Maloney or is it Malone like your brother?" Mama asked playfully.

"I say Maloney, Vincent says Malone. Doesn't much matter. We're blood just the same and I'm proud to call you my sister." He approached Mama and kissed her hand.

I gave him a growl to make sure he knew I was there and watching him. Then he pulled a bone from his pocket and gave it to me. "Here you go little fellow. I brought a bone for you this time." How could I disapprove of him now? A big, cooked, marrow-filled bone just for me. This was my favorite treat.

The men started to load each wagon with equipment from Mama's workshop. As the day wore on, it felt like the whole house was emptied into these wagons. One wagon was for personal effects. We would be gone for almost two seasons so much of our clothing and personal items must go. The second wagon was for the set up of the booth. Backdrops, demonstrations, parts, engravings, tables, and everything else a booth could need. The last wagon was for us to travel in.

As the light left the sky, the first two wagons were loaded and ready to go. They would start off in the morning. We would follow in a week in the third wagon.

Everything went as planned till it was our day to leave.

On the morning we were to leave, the great steam bell rang again. I barked my disapproval of someone interrupting our happy family, but Mama went to the door.

As she opened it, a very young man yelled, "The liberty will never die. Death to steam!" And he threw a brass ball into the entryway and ran back down the stairs. I ran after him growling and barking him away. When I was satisfied he was gone, I turned for home. At that moment, Daddy ran right past me, tossing the bright, shiny orb towards the young man. Readying his long gun, Daddy shot at the orb, setting off a huge explosion.

"That will show those Westies!" He shouted down to me. "It's the love of steam!"

Returning home, Mama looked worried. "Thank God you're safe." She said hugging Daddy. "I don't know what is wrong with them."

"Some rebels don't like technology. They find it scary to their world. The faster we get out of here the better and safer."

Daddy looked at Mrs. Baxter and asked sternly, "Is the house ready?"

"Yes Sir. Mrs. Worthington has the house till we return. And Mr. Gage will be staying here to make sure no one does anything to our home."

"Good!" Daddy said assuredly. "Darling, are you ready to be the belle of the technology ball?"

"I'm ready to show the world the smallest engines and what they can do!"

"Then Ladies, let us go to our wagon and off to Philadelphia." Daddy announced.

Mama grabbed me up and off we went in the big caravan of steam carts.

*****

The trip was very nice and much more comfortable that a normal wagon. We saw no rebels or had any attacks but people stared at us everywhere we went. At each stop to rest or refuel, eat, or relieve ourselves, people would come out of nowhere just to see our cart and ask questions. Most had never even heard of steam technology, much less seen it.

As we pulled into Philly, the wagons we had sent ahead had already arrived. The men had almost everything set up. Mama was so happy to see her work being displayed in a positive way that she had a hard time holding back the tears.

Daddy held her and kissed her on the head. "I told you I would make you famous."

"Thank you." Mama whispered back.

The expo was a great success. I got treats almost every day. Mama and Daddy built legs for four different people. Everybody knew the name Dr. Tapp and her miracle limbs.

Mama had kept her promise. Daddy had kept his. And the world now had a way to move about just a little bit easier.

*On the Scent of the Witch is the second fascinating Jean
Rabe story in this anthology. It gives us a different ending
to a tragic period in United States history. This story first
appeared in* Familiars (DAW Books).

On the Scent of the Witch

by Jean Rabe

There were lots of smells this bright spring morning–all
coming at a wonderful, dizzying pace, all pushed by the
strong wind that whipped across the field and fluttered the
wildflowers and teased her graying hair.

She breathed deep and held it for as long as she could,
picking through all the scents and settling on what had to
be her very favorite at this time of year–earth that recently
had been turned over. Planting time. Dark with moisture
from the rain two days past, it was filled with delightful
things–husks of beetles that had died when the cold hit,
pieces of rotted cornstalks striped with mold, smears that
had been tomatoes, wriggling masses of red worms and
more. Oh gloriously more!

Edging forward, she tipped her head this way and that,
letting the breeze play across her brow and letting it bring
still more smells her way. Something…yes, there was
something that stood out from everything, something that
caught and held her attention as sure as any vise.

Luck, what amazing luck! She inhaled again and headed toward what must be a most amazing treasure. Closing, as she seemed right on top of it now, she brushed aside one clump of dirt after another and another, moving a few feet and working at it some more, relentlessly, until she discovered part of a rabbit–the plump hindquarters. Indeed, an amazing find! It had been frozen over the winter, but was now nicely and thoroughly thawed. She sniffed at it, tail gently wagging when she noted just how pleasantly pungent it was. Had it been cut in half by a farmer's tool? Had a fox caught it in the fall, taking only what it wanted to eat at the moment and leaving the rest? No matter. Fortune was hers that no one else had come by earlier to claim this!

With a happy yip she fell on what was left of the carcass, rolling and twisting first on her back then on each side to smear the odor deep into her fur. She felt the dampness of the ground against her, bits of cornstalks scratching at her in just the right places. Looking up while she continued her gyrations, she spotted birds flying overhead. Oh, to give chase along the ground! She almost gave into the urge. But she was a smart dog, and she knew that there would be more birds coming along at any minute. There were always more birds. And she was an old dog, one who didn't run much anymore because she tired easily. Besides, she wanted to continue rubbing against the rabbit a little while longer, take as much of the smell away with her as she could, make sure she got it on her rump and legs, a little on her neck and….

She heard another dog bark, concentrating as she rolled more slowly now and trying to picture who was making the racket. Hathorne's dog perhaps? The big black brute was a noisy one, frequently barking only to hear itself. She hoped he wasn't headed this way to steal her treasure. Or maybe it was the sleek-coated yowler living at the bottom of Gallow's Hill. He was always fenced in near the sheep pen.

A most friendly dog, he only had freedom when with her help he could work the gate latch open. Or it could be....

With a disappointed whine she stopped her musings, feeling a presence stir at the back of her mind and forcing her to thrust aside all thoughts of the unidentified barker and the pungent rabbit. It was always the same when John intruded this way–a tickling sensation, that despite the number of times and through the number of years he'd done it, still gave her a curious feeling. Not an unpleasant one, and not close to the satisfaction of a good rub behind the ears, but something in between. There was something that was oddly soothing about it, the presence of her man John, who found her as a stray ten winters past and took her into his home and let her sleep on a thick rug by the hearth.

After a moment John took a more prominent position in her mind.

Where are we going? she asked him.

"To the church, Keesh," he answered. Though he spoke the words aloud in his cabin a half-mile away she heard them as clearly as if he were standing in front of her. "To see what visiting Cotton's up to."

She slowly rolled off the rabbit and shook until a stubborn clump of dirt dropped off her stomach. Then she gave an exaggerated wag of her plumy tail, happy to be doing something important for John. Keesh dutifully headed across the field and to the dirt street that ran through the middle of Salem, adopting a quick pace–or what was relatively fast as far as her advanced years were concerned. She reluctantly passed by the baker's, cocking her head to better pick up the smells of fresh bread and other delicacies.

In his cabin, John Broadmore looked out through the mongrel Keesh's eyes and at the same time inhaled the scents of cinnamon and apricots and melting butter. He concentrated and felt the dirt beneath the dog's paws.

"We will stop back at the bakery later, Keesh," he told her. "And we'll beg for a suitable treat. You're a smart dog. You're a very good dog."

John sat on an old wooden bench in front of a low table that was covered with chicken feathers dipped in fat, sand he had painted various colors, a bowl of dried ewe eyeballs, and a jar of whiskey that held the corpse of an unborn piglet. A thick book was in the midst of all of this, opened to the middle where his fingers danced over symbols that none in this town save he could translate. It was an old book, older than John, older than Salem and written long before the first Englishman came to this new world. Passed down from his father and grandfather and great-grandfather–who was said to have obtained it from a clueless Spanish merchant–it was a book of incantations, most of which John had mastered and several of which he indulged in the casting of daily.

John was the only practicing witch in the town, likely in the entire state of Massachusetts, and he'd hoped his work would have gone unnoticed. He had tried to be secretive, his altering the weather in the span of minutes–late at night when most folks were in bed and couldn't see the dry lightning, his causing corn crops to flourish in droughts or to wither unexpectedly in the passing of a day, his tinkering in the lives of neighbors to make them fall in and out of love for his entertainment, his manipulations to make the Newton boy steal and bully his friends.

And all the spells were cast through his familiar Keesh, the mongrel he'd taken such a liking to. "You're a clever dog," John mused. "A smart dog."

And all the spells were cast when John was safely inside his cabin with the doors and shutters locked, as they were now. All of the enchantments coming easier to him with each season. Making him more powerful and tying him more securely to the Art. He didn't even need the book for some of them, so expert he had become. The one that linked himself to the mongrel was second nature, and sometimes he found himself staring out through the dog's eyes without having invoked the spell. Keesh had become an extension of himself, and she was just this moment rounding the corner near the church, heading to the back where there was a stack of boards just under a window. Jumping up on them and peering through streaked glass, Keesh and John, through her eyes, watched a florid-faced man scribbling at a desk.

"Cotton Mather," John hissed through tightly clenched teeth. He let a breath escape, sounding like steam rising from a kettle left too long on the fire. "Damn him," he cursed, as his fingers turned one page and then another. His fingers danced faster. "Damn the man to the belly of Hell." John hadn't a spell that would do that, but he sometimes fancied taking a trip south where it was rumored a French woman brewed concoctions that would handle the job. "Vicious Cotton Mather."

Cotton Mather was why John had moved to Salem. Cotton Mather and his own curiosity. Mather was a frequent visitor to the place and had published a book recently, last year or the year before that John believed, 1691 or 1690. No. A few years earlier. It was called *Memorable Providences*, and it dealt with, among other things, an Irish washerwoman who lived in Mather's Boston and was suspected of being a witch. The book was popular and sold well, and John had two copies–one for posterity and one that he had marked up for research.

Mather, an influential Calvinist, took himself much too seriously and believed himself an authority on witches. "A subject he truly knows nothing about," John said. Nevertheless, there were germs of truth in what Mather penned–undoubtedly lucky speculation, and John decided that this most dangerous man had to stop inciting folks. John just hadn't settled on a way to stop him. Mather should stick to his study of science and his concern for the public health. He should leave the matter of witches alone. It would be healthier for him.

Keesha and John watched Mather for the better part of an hour, then listened intently as a stodgy assistant came in and eased himself into a nearby chair.

"The girls were at it again last night," the newcomer said. "Twitching and running around, hiding under the furniture. The smallest fell into a convulsion, and her father almost called for you. But it subsided soon enough."

Mather put down his quill and shook his head, his mop of curling white hair reminding Keesh of a cloud she spotted earlier. "Witchcraft," Mather pronounced. "No other explanation."

"Same as that child–Betty Parris," the assistant said. "Same as what happened to her this February gone."

Mather nodded and placed his hands on the table. Another shake of his head and he pushed his stool back and stood. "Horrible, Godforsaken witches. We will find them. And we will make them pay. We will chase the Devil out of Salem." As he walked to the window, Keesh scampered away.

John directed the mongrel to take a side street, one that went past the Parris house, where six-year-old Betty–one of Mather's study subjects lived. Indeed the child had suffered a convulsion and acted erratically, as had several other girls in Salem. A few whispered that the children were just trying to get attention or had caught some strange illness, though Mather and his cronies stood by their defense of witchcraft sitting at the heart of it all.

"Mather was right," John said. "Withcraft indeed." He spread some of the green sand and drew a design in it, then sprinkled a line of red sand beneath it. "But Mather will never understand just what it is all about." Keesh had visited Betty's home in February, and the child was quick to come outdoors and play with the friendly mongrel. Through Keesh, John had cast a spell that transferred his own essence, via the dog, into the child. John was experimenting with moving his mind from one body to the next and decided that children were the only vessels to consider at this juncture.

An adult might remember too much about the experience, might see John's face or draw the conclusion between the presence of John's mongrel and the episodes of fits. But a child...a child couldn't be entirely believed. They made up stories. They didn't understand things. To further help cloud the issue, John drew upon a simple incantation that passed the child a mild malady–and hence the brief convulsion. No harm done. No child injured. And John got closer in the process of being able to completely leave his body and enter another. With each passing month, he could do it for greater and greater periods of time.

The transference spell intrigued him, and it was the one he concentrated on above all others. He intended to use it– after he thoroughly mastered it, of course–to get himself a young, healthy body. But that would be a decade or two from now when this one began to ache and his senses began to grow feeble. He could not allow himself to succumb to the pitiful vagaries of old age, and then death, as his father and grandfather and great-grandfather had. There was too much magic to absorb in only one lifetime, and John wanted an opportunity to learn it all.

He shook off his thoughts and gazed through Keesh's eyes, seeing Betty playing in the yard with two other children. John smiled. The Jameson boy. The child was prone to exaggerating anyway. John flipped a page in the book, muttered a series of arcane phrases, and felt his mind pass from his body into Keesh, and then into the little boy.

The body in the cabin slumped forward, head cradled by the book.

The little Jameson boy kicked dirt at Betty and began running with glee. Keesh kept up with him for several minutes, yapping and jumping and delighting in the spring.

The trials started the following week.

*****

John hadn't intended for anyone to be hurt. He'd not injured a soul with his spells–not physically. And despite rough times, none of those he'd meddled with romantically divorced their spouses.

"No real harm had been done," he told himself. Keesh curled between his feet, he sat at his table, stirring sand and flipping pages in the book.

138

In late April several of the girls John and "borrowed" with his transference spell accused a former Salem minister of witchcraft. John hadn't planted the thought, didn't really know the poor man, and was at a loss to understand the girls' ramblings.

The following month more were arrested–examined and tried and hung.

"For no reason," John said. "Still, there's nothing to be done about it."

What could he do? he repeatedly asked himself. Tell Old Cotton Mather that those being strung up on Gallows Hill, and that the old man pressed by stones just yesterday, were not witches? That there were no witches in Salem save for himself? John knew if he confessed, he'd be hung. And there was too much magic in the world to master for that to happen. He couldn't surrender his life–no matter the consequences.

And so he watched the hangings, with Keesh at his side. The dog forlornly saw people who had once showed kindness by petting her drop to their deaths, kicking until the last of their lives trickled away. John explained to the dog, as best he could when they were melded, that matters had gotten out of control. Despite that, he continued to practice his transference spell–though not as frequent as before.

*****

It was the end of summer when they came for John, on a day when the sun hung high in a cloudless bright sky.

Perhaps it was because the previous night dry lightning shot above the town, yellow-gold fingers arrowing away from where his cabin sat. Perhaps he hadn't locked all the shutters. The wind had been fierce that night. Or perhaps it had been the Jameson boy. He'd targeted the child a dozen times and only lately had been worrying that the boy's description of the witch involved in the incidents closely matched his own appearance.

Cotton Mather personally took John away, locked him in a cell, gave him little to eat, and questioned him repeatedly.

"Are you a witch?"

"No," John lied.

"Have you familiarity with the Devil."

John vehemently shook his head.

Mather trundled away. In the hallway, he announced there would be a trial in the morning–and a hanging before sunset. John heard Mather and his associates discussing the details, and he heard Keesh whimper from beyond the cell window.

"I don't need the book," John said. It had been confiscated. They'd left all the sand and the feathers, every dried animal organ he'd collected and carefully cataloged. They didn't know what to do with it all. But they took the precious book. "I don't need it."

John pressed his face against the wall, just under the window, stretched out with his mind as he muttered a string of incomprehensible words, and felt his consciousness slip into the mongrel's body. This time, he pushed the spell to the limits of his ability.

*****

Keesh woke with a start, lying on a dirt floor inside a cell, lying in an unfamiliar body. With a sniff she knew it was John's body, knew what her man had done–she'd participated in so many of his spells to understand that he had mentally traded places with her. And though she didn't understand why he'd done this, she accepted it. She crawled on all fours to the door and barked, the sound strange coming from John's mouth. Keesh pulled herself up, weaving back and forth on two legs that threatened to crumble beneath her. Four legs were so much better for balance.

She barked again and again until the jailer came, and she kept barking until he opened the cell, frantic at what could be happening to his prisoner. Keesh barked once more as she bolted from the small building, ran across the street and toward John's cabin. Though unused to this form, she quickly mastered it. She was a smart dog. She delighted in its speed and its youth, and she threw back her head and let the breeze play with her hair as she hurried along.

Unfamiliar with fingers, she fumbled at the door for several minutes before she could get everything to cooperate. She shut the door behind her. Then after pacing the room for several minutes, smelling her own scent and John's heavy in the air, she lay down on the rug and slept. It was shortly before midnight that she arose, an idea stirring at the back of her mind. She was a smart dog.

The fingers were easier to manipulate now, and having two feet was posing little problem. Standing on John's toes, Keesh stretched a hand up to a top shelf and began pulling down colored sand and feathers.

She was indeed a very smart dog.

*****

The gray mongrel had been caught shortly after John's escape from jail. The old dog was headed toward the edge of town, running as fast as it could–which wasn't particularly fast given its age. Before sunset it was presented to Cotton Mather.

"Witch dog," someone pronounced. "Creature of the devil."

The mongrel's eyes were wide with fright. From inside the animal's shell, John tried to scream. But only a mournful howl escaped.

"Aye, it is a witch dog," Mather agreed. "A devil dog." He proceeded to go into great detail on how dogs were familiars of witches, agents of the devil and easily magicked. Since they could not have John Broadmore, they would have his dog.

They hung it the next morning.

*****

Cotton Mather tended to the ceremony himself, placing the noose about the frightened animal's neck. He thrust out the cries of the children to leave the animal alone. Only the young Jameson boy championed the execution.

When the animal was dead, and when he'd ordered it to be buried, he returned to the church and went straightaway to the back room. There, he dug about in an old chest that was filled with all manner of books and jars and bundled sheets of parchment. He pulled out one book in particular, a very old one filled with symbols that only he could translate. He turned to the transference spell and decided he would use it in another town, one that hadn't had trouble with witches and overzealous Calvinists. He'd find himself a better body, a younger one. Cotton Mather's was too old for his tastes, though he was grateful that Keesh had managed to switch his and Cotton's minds before the execution.

"A good dog," he breathed.

He would have to find himself another one, a mongrel. But before that, he'd end all these witch trials and hangings.

*****

Keesh stood next to a willow birch at the edge of Salem. She'd watched her dog body being hung, knowing Cotton Mather was deep inside it. The man would trouble no one again. She watched John, in Cotton's form, trundle off to the church. And she'd seen him turn at the last moment, looking to the woods, catching sight of her and smiling.

"You're a smart dog," she saw him mouth. "A very good dog."

Keesh smiled and stretched and turned north, well accustomed to this new two-legged form now. The early fall wind was bringing a myriad of smells her way–damp fallen leaves, a patch of earth covered with thick moss, and something amazing. Weaving through the trunks she strained to catch the odor, frustrated that these senses were not quite as keen as what she'd had before.

No matter, with patience she found it. There, beneath a large oak, was a dead bird–a big crow all swollen. It was not more than a few days dead, and it was pleasantly pungent. She dropped down on it and began to roll.

Historical note: In Salem, Massachusetts, in 1692, a man named John Bradstreet was charged with being a witch. He escaped and hid in the woods, but they caught a dog he supposedly used to give others "the evil eye," and hung it instead.

Dragons aren't always the man-eating lizards painted in myth. R'Marlee is a literary hug to one of the least known yet most brilliant men of the last century. Richard Marley is a quiet man who invented so many things, like the floppy drive, that made so many other technologies and technological breakthrough possible. He is indeed a wizard among men. And he really did get the damsel.

R'Marlee

by Joy Ward

CRACK! THUNK!

Prince Andrew crawled out from under the newly formed pile of lumber that until a few minutes before had been an ancient elm tree. His once fine brown linen breeches and blue silk tunic were now no more than rags in waiting. Fortunately, the next in line to his father's throne was young so he was just bruised and not broken. But he would be sitting gingerly on his horse for a few days.

Andrew threw his shoulder length chestnut hair back from his unusually dirty face. His somewhat scraggly young man's beard was festooned with leaves and small branches (and the occasional six-legged denizen who had been living it's peaceful life in the elm).
\Andrew was quite a sight but not one that would have pleased his fastidious mother. Queen Lydia wasar and wide for her fashion and beauty. This tableau looked more like a scene from a drunken brawl with a forest than a regal Prince.

Fortunately for him, no one was there to see his disrepair except his best friend and official companion, Rob, who stood outside the lumber pile barely able to maintain a straight face. One hand on his dark leather clad hip and the other across his mouth did little to assuage Andrew's chagrin. "Andrew, should I get your horse so we can return home or would you like to try something else ill-advised?" They had been friends a long time and Rob took certain liberties.

Andrew gave the other young man a scowl and got off his knees, trying ineffectually to knock debris off his clothes. "Thank you, Rob, for your deep concern. Yes, I am relatively unharmed."

Rob shook his blonde hair. "Now, can we move on to more potentially useful solutions to your problem? You have at this point consulted twelve magicians, none of whom have been able to help you. And this one just about got you killed with his misfiring spell. Are you ready to try something else?" Rob fixed his blue eyed stare on Andrew, waiting for him to respond.

"No need to remind me we are no closer to solving the conundrum of how to rescue Princess Shirley from the dire Dragon. All of these magicians swore they could get me to the top of Dragon Mountain and none have done it. But I must get there. How am I ever to be a respected Prince if I can't perform a simple damsel rescue? Rob, I simply must face and best this dragon or be the laughing stock of the other princes."

Rob patted his friend on his shoulder. "Yes, your Highness. There must be a way to do this without sacrificing your body or dignity. We will find a way. After all, if that wimpy Prince Woodrow of Lake-by-the-Deer-Field could rescue Princess Margery from an overgrown lizard like the dragon he out-talked, certainly we can find a way to rescue Princess Shirley."

The two men sank down on a newly fallen log. The forest around them seemed to have been stunned into a momentary silence when Andrew had been propelled by the last magician's not very effective spell a short distance from his manor into the un- offending elm. The planned destination had been Dragon Mountain a few miles away, looming over the forest. The idea was that the magician would use his magic to send Andrew through the air to the top of the mountain where he would confront the Dragon and sweep Princess Shirley off her feet. The mountain was unscaleable by normal means. The sides were simply too steep. Proof of that were the few but silently eloquent skeletons littering its base. Princing was a dangerous business, especially if the Prince in question had more bravado than sense.

Rob looked up with a thought dancing in his eyes.
"Andrew, there is one wizard we haven't tried..."
"Do you mean?..."
"Yes…"

"You must be joking! Everybody knows he's not quite right!"

"But, Prince, we have tried everybody else. And we're out of potential princesses to rescue. There are precious few damsels left in distress. You're almost down to rescuing pre-teens like Princess Brie."
Andrew shivered in disgust. "oh no! Pre-teen princesses give me the willies! They just stand there, not talking and looking like everything in the world disgusts them. No,

before, I do that I will seriously consider unmarried bliss and adopting my heir. If I wait long enough, Queen Mother will give up on me giving her a grandchild."

"You don't really believe that do you, Andrew?" Rob sat, studying the Prince with a cocked eyebrow. "Sounds like a rationalization to me."

The previously quiet forest was stirring back into activity around them. Several squirrels rushed overhead in some still standing fir and other evergreen trees. Birds chittered elsewhere in the high limbs and the sound of a woodpecker in search of his afternoon meal echoed through the woods. Rob sat, watching the Prince consider his lack of options. They were few. He could go home where the Queen would continue to harangue the Prince about his duties to family and country. He could throw himself on the pile of already whitened bones at the foot of Dragon Mountain or he could take desperate measures and consult the wizard, R'Marlee. No one had seen R'Marlee for some time, which considering his proclivity for getting in bar fights, was considered a good thing by the local barkeeps. But perhaps the scariest thing about wizard R'Marlee was how he got things done. He did not use magic. Oh no, he used what he called "technology."

Where magicians trained in alchemy and astrology, R'Marlee used extremely arcane knowledge like mathematics and the dreaded physics! Not even other wizards could understand him when he got talking. Most of them would pretend to listen but you could see their bespectacled eyes begin to glaze over and soon they would find reasons to slip out of the room. One might have to feed the pigs or another might be in need of shopping for an anniversary present for his wife. The crowd may have been fairly large in the beginning but before too long it would have dwindled to a handful of poor souls who could not think fast enough to find an excuse to escape.

R'Marlee was simply too erudite for most of the other wizards. Even the ones who could understand him feared his sharp tongue. He had little patience for mental dawdlers. He had been known to remove a top layer of skin with a few well chosen, scathing words from a prince who had asked some inane question.

This was the wizard that Rob suggested they ask for help. Yes, R'Marlee was more nightmare threat than potential savior but if there was no other choice...

After sitting in shared silence for a few more minutes Prince Andrew seemed to come to some internal decision. He stood up, flicking away another bug he had found in his hair, and reached over, offering Rob his outstretched hand. "Come along, Rob. The day is late and we must return to the castle to eat and rest. Tomorrow, we face R'Marlee."
His face looked as grim as if he were considering wrestling a full grown, rather hungry bear.
Rob, not wanting to push his luck, ro
se silently and dusted off his breeches and leather jerkin.
"As you say, your highness."

The two men proceeded back to the castle where they spent the night eating, resting and hiding the prince's numerous scars from his somewhat over protective mother.
The next morning, Prince Andrew and Rob set out on their horses to find R'Marlee. No one seemed to know exactly where he lived so the two men followed what rumors they got at the lodges and inns along their path.
They rode for several days, stopping each night at inns that could offer food and shelter to them and their mounts. At each stop, they asked after the famed wizard, garnering just

enough information to keep moving in what they presumed to be the right direction.

Soon, they reached the end of the fairly civilized path, coming to something not much more than a path trod by deer. The horses could get through the woods with them for another day when it became clear the path was angling up a small mountain, through almost impassable woods.

The men were wondering if they were on the right path when they came to a small shepherd's hut. Rob climbed off his horse and knocked on the rough-hewn door.
An older man dressed in homespun cloth opened the door. His grey hair peaked out from under a green wool hat while his unkempt beard fought for space on the man's lined face. "Hallo, youngsters! What brings you here? Are you lost or in need of a sheep?"

"Hopefully neither, respected father. We seek a wizard." Rob stood on the porch, eying the old shepherd.
"Then ye be in the wrong place." He made to shut the door.
"Wait, sir. Do you know of the wizard R' Marlee?"
The lined face paled just enough for Rob to notice. "I might. What is it to ye?"

"We've come quite a way to speak with him. We would greatly appreciate it if you could help us find him."

About that time four large black dog faces appeared behind and around the shepherd. Rob backed up with a gasp. "Will they attack me?" He was already wondering how he would ever get away from these huge dogs if they came after him. "Not unless you are a damn fool. Are you, a damn fool that is?"

The dogs continued to silently stare at Rob through the doorway, moving neither forward or back. Their gold eyes reading his every move.

"I hope not, sir." Rob was beginning to feel the beginning of a need for a privy. The intense canine stares seemed to have that effect on his plumbing.

"Then what need have ye of this wizard? Does he owe you money? Did he steal your woman? You've come a long way it seems for some reason. I'll tell you nothing until I know why you want him." The man seemed to get just a bit taller, filling the doorway. And did his clothing seem a bit cleaner and newer?

Rob swallowed. If he told this man nothing their search was ended. They were at a dead end. "Well, sir. It's like this. My friend there is Prince Andrew and he is trying to find a way to rescue Princess Shirley who is currently being held by a dragon. The problem is that the dragon lives on a very high mountain so he needs help getting to the top. That is why we seek the venerable wizard R'Marlee." "There are other wizards, many of whom are quite friendlier than old R'Marlee." The man reached down to pet the dark head of the nearest dog.

"We've dealt with them. They may be friendlier but they are, to be polite, not as smart or learned."

The man grinned at that. "You're right there, young man." He looked back at the still intensely silent dogs and thought for a minute. "What think you, Socrates, Pythagoras? What about you, Plato, Angle, should we let them in?"

Rob's eyes opened a bit wider. "Are you R'Marlee?" He could not believe their luck.

"Some call me that. Others have called me other things or names, usually fairly unfriendly and unflattering." He laughed at his own joke and waved the four huge black dogs back from the door.

"May we come in, sir?" Now that a Rob knew he was talking with the famed wizard he knew to be even more polite. It never paid to irk wizards, especially when they were the last hope for your liege's happiness.

"Angle, Py, and the other dogs seem to have nothing against you so I guess so. At least until you prove yourselves to be damn fools." With that he reached out, petting one of the dogs then opening the door a bit wider. "Excuse me a minute." Rob walked back out to where Andrew sat on his horse.
"We have found him, Andrew. Come on!"
Andrew looked doubtful. "This is the wizard? Are you teasing me? This is a shepherd's hut. Surely no great and powerful wizard would live here!"

Rob sighed. He had been like a brother to the Prince but sometimes Andrew could be such a snob! Now was not the time! If R'Marlee felt Andrew was not worthy to help what would they do?

"Andrew, get off the horse and come in. And be polite!" Rob practically hauled Andrew off the horse and into the small house.

What a shock when they walked through the wooden doorway! The inside was much bigger on the inside than it appeared on the outside! It was a spacious cottage with fine furniture and plaster walls. The large foyer led directly into a massive room with fourteen foot ceilings. All around the room were bookcases reaching to the ceiling and long tables with bits and pieces of equipment. Light flooded in through skylights set into the ceiling.

He had never seen anything like it! Rob stood gawking like a farm boy on his first trip to the fair.

Andrew,trying to appear princely and in charge, pushed down his own amazement. "So you are the legendary R'Marlee?" He asked. Andrew tried to look like he interacted with the unexpected everyday and twice on Sundays.

"I think we have agreed on that." The wizard frowned slightly and Rob hoped he wasn't considering turning them out for being "damn fools."

Rob quickly decided to intervene. "Venerable wizard, will you consider helping us?" He hoped Andrew had the good sense to hold his tongue.

"I don't see a good reason to. Can you give me one?" The wizard seemed to have gotten even taller and younger. His white hair had darkened to deep brown.

Rob wondered if it was a trick of the light or had the wizard done something. No matter, right now. Back to the Dragon and Princess Shirley...

"Money?" Rob offered.

"I have plenty for what I need and no wish to fool with dragons." The wizard pulled a large purple bound tome off a bookcase and began flipping through it.

"The kingdom's thanks and well wishes?"

"P'shaw, I care even less for that." R'Marlee continued looking at his book.

Rob was beginning to despair of ever marrying off the Prince. "What do you want? What can we offer you?" The tall wizard closed his book and looked up at Rob. "That is the first smart question you have asked. I will not tell you what I want now but you must promise that the Prince will grant me one wish when the deed is done."

"Prince Andrew, what do you say?" Rob turned back to where Andrew stood, trying desperately to look very royal but failing miserably.

"You want me to promise you who knows what?" The Prince's shocked expression sent Rob leaping to his side. In a harsh whisper, he reminded Andrew what was at stake. "Prince, stop and think! He is your last hope!"

The Prince closed his mouth, biting down the words trying to escape.

Rob swung back to R'Marlee. "Can we put some limits on this arrangement? You know, something like no first born children, that kind of thing?"

The wizard gave an enigmatic small smile. "I will tell you this. What I ask you for you will be willing to give. Is that surety enough?"

Rob pulled Andrew back toward the door. "Andrew, how does this sound to you? He says he will ask you for something you will not want." Inwardly, Rob was twisting his shirt in anxiety. If Andrew didn't accept these terms Rob had no backup plans.

Andrew hemmed, hawed and scuffed his shiny boots on the not very shiny tiled floor. R'Morlee continued to look through the books on the bookshelf as if only the dogs watched him. The only other sounds came from behind. One of the large, short-haired dogs had fallen into a light sleep complete with resounding snores.

Just when Rob thought he might faint from frustration, Andrew finally spoke.

"All right. I can agree to that but we must be very clear that you agree to get us to the top of Dragon Mountain, safely, and down again once I have vanquished the Dragon and rescued the Princess Shirley. What say you, wizard?"

Wizard R'Marlee continued to pick up and put back books for a few more minutes, saying nothing. Rob could hear the dog's snoring (he thought it was the one the wizard had called Py) and faint wind chimes on the front porch. He swore if this kept up much longer he would start to hear crickets as evening fell.

Wizard R'Marlee put down the red book he held, adjusted his gold-laced robes (Rob wondered when that had happened. Last he noticed the wizard was wearing cottons.) and looked Andrew squarely in the eyes.

"I say I agree to your terms. Please remember that I do this of my own free will, not as your serf or servant. Excuse me for a minute while I prepare to leave and ready the technology to fulfill your request." With that R'Marlee swung around and went through a door behind him to the left. The dogs, even the formerly sleeping one, jumped to attention at his heels. Two went with the wizard while the other two stood guard by the door, watching Andrew and

Rob as if they were steaks about to be abandoned on a dinner table. Neither man moved an eyelash.

A few minutes later R'Marlee stuck his head back into the large room. "Come on! Time's a'wasting."

The other two dogs followed him through the door as did the two young men, studiously watching the dogs move ahead of them.

They walked into an even larger room. The men could see the late afternoon light flowing through the skylights that made up the ceiling. This room was four times larger than the one they had just left.

The most amazing things in the room were machines and parts of machines sitting around the room. Some had seats, giving the idea one might sit in them. Other equipment was completely unreadable with no clue as to their uses.

Andrew glanced around but seemed to be completely unimpressed. His royal education had focused on princely things such as how to interact with other royals and look impressive seated on a throne or horse. Neither the King nor the Queen felt their son should learn much about science or, Fates forbid!, technology. Only the working classes needed to know those things so they could keep the grist mills moving or the ovens baking.
Rob was the son of a cooper so he actually knew what a hammer looked like and did. His eyes ran across the rooms and the stuff. He recognized some things but many others he had not. What was the wizard doing here? Rob promised himself that once all this was over he would return and learn about all these things.

"Do either of you have a fear of heights?" R'Marlee was

standing next to large cage with four paddles on top, like a fan. There were four seats inside the cage.

"I guess not." Rob had no problem climbing the highest trees near the castle. He didn't know about the prince but it was not correct to admit his liege feared anything. After all, how high was the wizard talking about? It couldn't be that high.

"Good to hear." With that, the wizard, who somehow had changed back to his cotton pants and shirt, walked to the wall where he grabbed a hank of rope and pulled.

Rob heard a creaking and looked up to see the glass ceiling rolling back, revealing the room to the clear sky. Both young men gasped. Andrew looked like he might run until Rob placed a restraining hand on the prince's arm. "Prince, calm! This is just technology. We are safe."

The Prince took a deep breath. "You are right, Rob. This is all part of saving Princess Shirley. We must be brave." "Ready to go. All in." R'Marlee climbed in the front left seat and buckled a belt across his lap. "Are you going or staying with the dog pack. I don't mind taking you there but it is not my job to defeat the dragon."

Under his breath, R'Marlee mumbled. "Besides I quite like old Scaly. We've had a few good chess games."

The two younger men clambered into seats in the back of the cage, fastening their own belts. The wizard turned a switch in front of him and the blades on the top of the cage began to rotate. They began slowly then sped up. The whole contraption vibrated.

The wizard turned slightly and said something the riders could not hear over the rotating blades.

Then, wonder of wonders, the cage began to lift off the ground.

"Rob, what is happening?" The prince's green eyes bulged with fear. He gripped the metal sides of the cage as if it were going to fall away at any time.

Rob, on the other hand, was exhilarated! They were rising in the air! Could anything be more exciting? No one would believe him. He felt a huge grin spread across his windblown face.

R'Marlee seemed to be completely comfortable piloting the flying cage.

Rob heard Andrew gag next to him. When he turned in the prince's direction he caught him wiping his mouth with his right sleeve.

"Just a touch of, um, stomach upset."
Rob gave a sympathetic smile and patted Andrew's arm. Then Rob went back to watching the land pass beneath them.

Soon, the cage landed on the top of Dragon Mountain. None too soon for Andrew, it seemed who could not unbuckle his belt and clamber out of the still vibrating cage any faster. Rob was not far behind him.

"Here you are, princeling. Top of the mountain and there's the dragon"s cave." R'Marlee gestured toward the very obvious and impressive cave in front of them.

"Look at that view, Andrew! Isn't it wonderful?" Rob tried to pull Andrew closer to the edge but the prince was having none of it.

"We should see to our task, Rob, not sight see." Andrew backed as far away as possible from the steep drop off over the edge.

R'Marlee grinned and got out of the cage. "Well, shouldn't we go in and announce ourselves? It's rude to stand outside gawking. Besides, I can't wait to see you vanquish Old Scaly and rescue the, uh, er, damsel." With that he strode toward the mouth of the cave.

"We can't let the old wizard beat us to the dragon, now can we, Andrew." Rob subtly but definitely drug his friend after the wizard.

The dark cave became larger and brighter as the trio walked further in.

At first, they could only hear water dripping from the cave ceiling. Soon, they began to hear two raised voices.

They walked further into the cave where they began to notice the cave was, dare they say it, decorated? There were nicely formed windows with chintz curtains. There was softly upholstered human-sized furniture. Oil and pastel landscapes hung on the walls. Here and there small china statues decorated wall shelves.

Moving further into the surprising cave it became apparent the sources of the voices. An immense green dragon, maybe seventy feet tall standing in front of them was holding a broom. The ceiling of the cave reached high over

159

him. Around his waist was a khaki apron. Standing further in the cave, in her own khaki apron tied over a purple dress, was a petite thirtyish woman. Her long sandy brown hair was piled atop her head, allowing the trio to see her very pretty face, which, at the moment, was set in a determined look as she gave the dragon an intense glare.

"Yes, dear, I AM sweeping. Yes, light of the world, I am listening to you." The immense dragon nodded as he swept through the cave. His steely claws wrapped around the immense broom.

R'Marlee strolled in and took a seat in a beige recliner, near the entry, obviously making himself at home.
Andrew turned to Rob. "What do I do now?"
Rob shook his head. "I guess you should challenge the dragon. R'Marlee will get anxious to leave soon."

"You're right," Andrew said. He turned toward the still sweeping dragon. "Uh, Sir Dragon, I am here to vanquish you and rescue the fair damsel in distress. I hope this does not come to blows." Truth be told, Andrew was not the best warrior and avoided fights when possible.

The dragon turned to the young men for the first time as if just noticing their presence. "Really, you are here to challenge me for Shirley? Did I hear you correctly, small monkey?"

Andrew shuffled his feet and glanced at Rob. "Yes, I am here to do my princely duty."

About that time, the princess who had been momentarily quiet, spoke up. "Dragon, are you trying to get out of sweeping the cave by talking with these strangers?" Her tone was none too welcoming.

The dragon stood the much larger than normal broom against the cave wall. His face wrapped in a huge grin that revealed quite a few rather sharp teeth. "Princess, did you not hear? This young man has come to rescue you. Are you not excited to be freed from your captivity?" If Rob was not mistaken he might think the dragon seemed relieved. R'Marlee chuckled.

Andrew pulled Rob to the side. He whispered to his friend. "Does the dragon sound, uh, happy?"

Rob shrugged. "Quite strange. I thought by now he would be trying to fry you."

Then the cave shook and a massive thump resounded as the dragon fell dramatically on his back. " I admit you have bettered me, Prince, uh, what is your name?"

"Andrew..."

The dragon continued. "Ah, Prince Andrew, you have defeated me. I must release the Princess Shirley to you. Did you hear me, Shirley? You are required to go with the young Prince who has vanquished me. Uh, that means your dogs, Baby and Duffy as well."

"Finally, some prince had enough guts to face you. It's been what, twenty years in this cave? Duffy, Baby, where are you? Come to Mama!"

About that time, two dogs ran in and over the prone dragon. One dog was a smallish white dog and the other a black dog that looked just like the Wizard's. R'Marlee gave a quite un-wizardly guffaw.

Andrew looked around like a pike on a hook. Rob could tell Andrew was starting to look close to running for the flying cage and escape. Oh no! They had come too far to not rescue Princess Shirley. What was happening here?

"Andrew, calm down. Breathe. You have vanquished the dragon and rescued the damsel. You can go home proudly."

"Yes, Rob, but look how old she is! She must be almost forty! I thought she would be younger! I can't marry an old woman who bosses around a dragon! Help me!"

Rob felt a tap on his left shoulder.

"May I cut in?" R'Marlee stood behind him, a broad smile on his face.

"Um yes. What..." Rob never got to finish his question.

"Now would be an appropriate time to tell you what I require for my payment to assist your prince."

"What, now? Really is this the best time? We have, um, a situation here that..."

"Yes, young man, you do. I am going to relieve your burden. I claim the fair princess Shirley as my payment."

Had Andrew heard the wizard correctly? "You want Shirley?" Andrew's voice rose at the end of the sentence.

"Yes. I told you at the beginning that I would require a prize you would not want. Does the young prince want to marry Shirley?"

"Um, he has great respect for the Princess but I think I can safely say that no, he does not. But, Wizard, can you please explain all of this to me?"

"Let us go back outside."

Rob and R'Marlee went back to the mouth of the cave.

"Now, Wizard, please explain. Why is the dragon so determined to relinquish Shirley? Why have no other princes rescued her? And why do you want her? I am terribly confused."

"You have seen how high the mountain is, have you not?" The Wizard winked at Rob.

"Uh, yes. So?"

"The mountain is too steep for anyone to scale without my help. The Dragon thought Shirley would be here a week or so before a prince came to salvage her honor. She had to be rescued by a prince or risk being laughed out of the princess club. It's quite embarrassing for a princess to be rescued from a dragon by anyone else."

"Wouldn't you help them?"

"No, none would agree to my payment."

"And..."

"A little known fact is that Shirley and I had been, er, stepping out before her time with the dragon."

"So why didn't you rescue her?"

"As I said before, young man, Shirley refused to be rescued by anyone other than a prince. It just would not do. Now, I have answered your questions and we should return to your friend before he gets in trouble."

The two men went back into the cave where Andrew, the dragon and Shirley were sharing a nice bottle of Pinot Noir.

The dragon was making a toast with his very large wine-filled glass. "Here is to a new life for everyone!"

Shirley gave R'Marlee a distinctly coy look and blushed. "Are you ready for some serious arm-wrestling, Wizard? Best two out of three buys the next round. That little pub with all the leather is still open, isn't it?"
Andrew and Rob shared a look of surprise while the dragon coughed out a harsh laugh and R'Marlee grinned.

Princess Shirley reached over and gave Prince Andrew a hug and a chaste kiss on the cheek. "I do appreciate you coming to rescue me but I think this is the best for everyone, don't you? Besides, I always did have the hots for brainy men. No offense…"

With that she stepped over to R'Marlee and gave him a pat on the behind.

Loneliness can make all beings reach across species lines to find friends. Sometimes Natures Sleeps was written when a publisher asked me to write a dragon story. I pooh-poohed the idea antil he told me I could add a dog. The story first appeared in Dragons Composed (Kerlak Publishing).

Sometimes Nature Smiles

by Joy Ward

Nature can be cruel. Grandmothers die. Puppies are stillborn. Little girls and dogs can feel that Nature has marooned them in their loneliness.

But sometimes Nature smiles and changes the rules of the game. Sometimes the lonely are comforted and dreams, even the most unlikely of dreams, come true.

The melting glacier let loose a shiny form to be carried into the wider snow-and-ice-covered world. How long the egg had lain in its crystalline rest we'll never know.

Certainly the polar bear mother and cub who tried to grab it in their hairy paws had never seen an egg quite like this one. Nor had the five young seals as they tossed it around among them and took turns balancing it on their noses. They knew the roundness and instinctively realized they wouldn't break it.

No, this was no usual egg. Never mind that few eggs floated loose from dissolving glaciers, this egg looked and felt very different than any other egg that had been seen under the bright glare of the arctic sun or anywhere else for that matter for thousands of years. This egg was about a foot long. The egg itself felt like rubber that maybe had been too long in the sun. If the seals could have talked they would have told you the surface was rather scratchy, the smell was somewhat sulphurous and oh, it was much too warm for a regular sort of egg. They probably didn't notice that the egg was a splotchy light brown to rusty red and all the shades in between.

And there was a sound deep inside this rather unusual egg that promised this was not a dead egg. Something lived in its warm, odiferous depths. Something old. Something much, much older than any of the furry witnesses watching its progress as it journeyed from its ancient hiding place to the world that had moved from ice to warmth so many times in so many millennia since this oh-so-unusual egg had been secreted inside a frozen mountain of water.

The seals could hear the sound. They called to it, recognizing it as something or someone they should know. They barked among themselves, asking if anyone could name that sound, or that animal. None could but all felt something familiar when they heard the sound. After a few hours of playing with the egg and calling to the egg, on the chance whatever was in it could come out and play, the seals let the egg float on its way, tossed by the current like it had been tossed by the seals.

Days passed as the egg bobbed up and down on the waves. Large fish nosed the egg, hoping for a meal. Orcas pushed the egg here and there, trying to decide if it was edible. All of them -- fish, sharks, and other sea mammals -- smelled the egg and decided this was something not worth the trouble. It wasn't that they thought there was nothing in the egg; they sensed the thing inside and made the decision to leave it alone.

You see, somewhere in the back of their brains they remembered the smell and the feel of this egg. Buried deep, deep in their hind brains was this smell and feel. And the smell and feel said in no uncertain terms, "Leave it alone!" If you could have asked the sharks why, of course they couldn't have said anything beyond, "Here is an old, old power that everything in my ancient body says is pure danger to the likes of me."

So the egg floated on. And the baby inside continued her dreams of fire and warm scales and flying.

As the egg floated south toward land, the baby's dreams began to recede. Just like her egg floated on the ever-moving waves, she began to float to her mind's surface as she got closer and closer to waking up. The ice was losing its grasp on her as she moved into warmer water.

Before long, the sounds and smells of the warm before birth gave way to the salt of the ocean and the cry of the gulls in the baby's dreams. Just as she was starting to realize that she was awake, her egg washed up on sand and rocks. She could still feel the waves lapping at her shell, but the tide was moving out. The baby had found a new home. This would be the first springtime to see the birth of a baby dragon in thousands of years.

But babies, even dragon babies, need more than just a place to have a home; they need a family. The baby's new family awaited her. Even now, as she moved inside the shell, stretching her muscles against the shell, her new family was getting closer and closer as they unknowingly ambled toward the egg.

Twelve-year-old Cassandra strolled along the beach, picking up unusual looking shells, examining them and then tossing most of them back to the rock-strewn beach.

She kept a few to add to her grandmother's garden. Cassandra loved her grandmother deeply and even though her Grand Mary had died just a few weeks ago, spending time in the ancient garden made her feel closer to her and not quite so lonely and lost. Her grandmother had been her best friend and the one person who seemed to understand Cassandra.

Cassandra had never had much patience with other children. She had preferred her grandmother's company and that of other species such as dogs and horses. Other children were too cruel, too insensitive to be of much interest to the young girl who spent most of her time in her grandmother's garden or listening to her grandmother tell tales of other times. So when Grand Mary died, Cassandra felt the light bleed from her life leaving her days dark and lonely.

Carolyn, Cassandra's mother, loved her daughter but she had a life to lead, money to make, a daughter to support. Her husband had died some years hence leaving Carolyn in her own darkness. She loved her daughter but as happens so often, they were not close.

The other member of the baby's new family was Beatrice, a female middle-aged Beagle who, if she could have spoken would have said she was feeling just as lonely as Cassandra (known as Cassie to almost everyone). Beatrice had delivered her last litter a few days ago and the one puppy had been stillborn. Bea, as Cassie called her, had forced out the puppy but knew as she licked and prodded the unmoving body that he would never suckle. Where there should be the happiness of puppy breath and snuggling babies, there was only the stench of death. Bea struggled against the depression that threatened to overwhelm her, even on a beautiful morning like this one was with the hope of enticing smells all around her on the beach and at her home where Cassie's mother fried eggs and baked biscuits for breakfast.

Beatrice hadn't really wanted to walk to the beach this day but her Cassandra asked her to come along. Bea realized that Cassie understood her grief and just wanted to make her feel a little better so she relented and took her place by Cassie's side. Besides, Bea knew that Cassie was still grieving and, even though she couldn't tell her she understood. Bea could be with her. Together, they could share their unspoken link, girl and dog.

Cassie had been raised around animals all her life. Her earliest memories included watching Beatrice's mother give birth to her and her sisters and brothers. Cassie helped her family with the chickens and horses, and even knew how to milk the two cows that kept the family in milk throughout the year. In short, Cassie would tell you that she loved animals of all types.

You see Cassandra didn't just feel the common sort of betwixt and between that most girls her age felt; caught between being too old to be a child and not quite old enough to be a teenager or young adult. Of course that didn't help. Cassie had always felt rather lost between her humanness and the rest of Nature. She never felt totally comfortable with children her age yet she felt completely at home with all kinds of other species. But there was one major problem. It had always been her greatest frustration that although she could touch her animal friends like Bea, she couldn't really know what they thought and felt. So she could talk with her own species, but didn't really want to and the very ones she wanted to most listen to, she couldn't.

So Cassie in her blue jeans, long sleeve green T-shirt and shoulder length light brown hair pulled up in a large clip watched Bea as she minced across the lapping waves that tossed themselves up on the beach with watery fingers pinching at the Beagle's paws. Both girl and dog felt weighed down by their losses, their loneliness made even worse by not being able to share their pain with the other.

But Nature was about to smile and change everything for all three of these lonely ones -- girl, dog and dragon.

Beatrice smelled the egg and ran ahead on the beach. She knew this was something much different than the usual animals and junk tossed up by the ocean. She wasn't quite sure what the smell was but Bea knew that it tickled something at the back of her brain, something telling her that this was much, much older than what looked like a rather large luminous egg. In her excitement she forgot once again that Cassie couldn't understand her Beagle vocalizations. Bea tried to tell her to hurry and see the shiny, ancient thing as she danced ahead of Cassie.

"Bea, slow down. What's got you so excited?" Cassandra could tell Bea was worked up about something but all she could hear were what sounded to her like the high-pitched baby cries that Beatrice voiced,

Beatrice's cries got louder because, just like Cassie felt frustrated by not being able to talk with Bea, Bea felt the same frustration. Bea so wanted to be able to tell Cassie what she knew and thought! And now here was an amazing new thing and she couldn't even tell Cassie about the delicious stink of the egg!

With Cassie following about fifteen feet behind, Bea reached the egg. She started sniffing at it and batting it with her front paws.

At the very moment Bea was filling her nose with the scent and feel of the egg, it cracked in two! Fearless as she was,

Bea stood her ground. The baby dragon looked at Bea with her huge sky blue eyes. Then the baby blinked and headed towards Bea, a scant foot or so away. Bea and the baby only saw each other. The rest of the beach was only background.

The baby dragon, who we'll learn to call Bridget like everyone else did, had never seen a grown dragon. Bridget saw Beatrice and from then on there was nothing that could have convinced Bridget that Bea was not her mother. Bea and Bridget, Beagle and dragon, instantly became mother and child.

Oh of course, Bridget would get bigger than Beatrice but love doesn't see those sorts of things as problems. Sure, Bea didn't smell like a dragon but that also was not a problem. Bea smelled and acted like a mom. And moms of all species know babies when they see them. Bea knew Bridget needed a mother and Bea was the best mother she knew.

Bea nosed the silvery baby dragon as the dragon used its bright blue eyes to drink in the world around her. Bridget was a baby female dragon born into a world that had not seen her kind in thousands of years. She had so much to learn but now she was not alone. She had a family.

Bea did what all new mothers know to do and cleaned up her new large baby with a studied insistence, licking off the light greenish afterbirth that clung to the hatchling.

Cassie came upon Bea cleaning Bridget while the early morning sun glinted off the shattered egg and the young dragon.

Cassie had seen dragons in the books lining her mother's library. There had been pictures of all sorts of dragons. The stories of dragons skipped through her mind. Their stories had been in histories all over the world – Europe, China, and so many more places. But she never expected to see one here, on her beach! And a baby one at that!

What would her mother say? Would she let her keep Bea's adopted pup? And what should she call the young dragon? Was it a pup or a cub or who knows? What should she do? She obviously couldn't leave the baby here on the beach. Sure, the dragon baby was bigger than the dogs and many other predators but this was a baby animal. She couldn't just walk off and leave the baby to starve or die in some other way on the beach. This was a baby and Cassie was not the kind of girl to abandon a baby animal.

Besides, Bea was fascinated with her new charge, licking and sniffing every inch of its leathery body. Cassie knew Bea well enough to know she couldn't leave the baby behind. Bea was not that kind of dog or mother.

As Cassie rifled through all her possibilities in her mind the young dragon seemed to see her for the first time. Bridget pulled her front left leg out of Bea's mouth and trundled toward Cassie. For the first time Cassie saw the dragon's eyes. Bridget's eyes were huge and a color a jeweler would call London Blue if they were gems. And they shone like gems! There were no eyelashes that Cassie could see but the lids quickly flicked over the eyes. There was more wing than body to the dragon, making her a bit unsteady. The tail was a little longer than the dragon's body with gradations of darker to lighter silver, ending in a flat arrow shape. In all, the young dragon with her silvery skin and vibrant blue eyes was more beautiful than the imaginary portraits in the fairy tale books. The sunlight seemed to halo the dragon's head as she turned her intense gaze on Cassie.

Bridget moved to about a foot from Cassie's right leg and gave her one long appraising look. Cassie wasn't sure how she knew it but somehow the hatchling was taking her measure. Bea hung back a bit as if to let Cassie and Bridget have a moment alone. Bridget leaned against Cassie's leg, keeping her eyes locked onto Cassie's. At that moment Cassie knew there was only one thing to do; Bridget was coming home with them.

What Cassie was to learn later was that the stories of talking dragons were not quite true; most couldn't talk to humans. Dragons didn't necessarily speak human language. Instead they, like many of the other species that came along after them, could communicate with some humans in other ways. The young dragon could reach the minds of those humans open and sensitive to other species. Cassie was one of these lucky people who could feel their thoughts and emotions. She knew her mother heard animals like the birds calling for food in cold weather and the dogs as they yearned to chase the nattering raccoons in the backyard. So the fact that she could feel the dragon's thoughts and emotions as they stood on the otherwise deserted beach that morning wasn't strange.

So this is how the first dragon to meet the sunlight in who knows how long came to join the family of Cassie and Beatrice.

It took somewhat longer to make the trek up from the beach to Cassie's home than it had coming down the gentle slope. The newborn dragon was learning how to walk while keeping her substantial wings and tail out of her way. Cassie encouraged Bridget from the front and Bea nudged her from behind. A few times a poorly placed rock would cause Bridget to struggle to maintain her balance but then Bea would find the place to shove the dragon baby to help her over the obstacle. Cassie considered picking the baby up and carrying her but somehow that didn't seem like the best idea. After all, the dragon could bite her and who knew what kind of damage even a newborn dragon could inflict?

As the threesome approached Cassie's back porch overlooking the path up from the ocean, Cassie began to wonder how to tell her mother about the family addition. Would her mother let her even keep the dragon? Her mother was a lot of good things but this was a stretch for anyone.

Cassie could hear her mother bustling around the kitchen and could smell breakfast. Bea and Bridget could too. Bridget started snorting and looking around to find the source of the interesting smells. The back door swung open and Cassie's mother, Carolyn, stuck her head out.

"Cassie, just in time for breakfast. You and Beatrice get in here before it all gets cold." Then she pulled her head back inside. She didn't notice Bridget. Yet.

"Mom, please come out here a minute." Cassie wanted her mother to meet Bridget in the open and not be surprised in her own kitchen. She hoped things might go better that way.

Carolyn came out the screen door, wiping her hands on a red kitchen towel. "What's up?" Then, before Cassie could say anything, her mother saw the dragon. The foot-long, silver dragon was leaning against the tri-color Beagle as if they had been mother and baby forever. Bea was licking Bridget's eyes and making low, murmurings. The sun glinted off the silver scales.

Carolyn's mouth dropped open. She glanced at Cassie and then back at the maternal tableau of dog and dragon. "Cassandra, explain!" She pushed back some stray brown hairs that had pulled themselves out of the clip holding the rest of her own shoulder length hair. Then her hands unconsciously started ruffling through the pockets set in the sides of her pants as if looking for some mislaid note.

Cassie reached up and pushed back some of her own hair that had fallen across her eyes. "It's a dragon and Beatrice has adopted it." She didn't know then that the baby was a girl and that her name was Bridget so she gave Carolyn all the information she had.

Cassie's mother was not amused. "I can tell this is a dragon but I'm betting there's a bit more to the story. Such as why there is a mythological creature sitting at my backdoor with my daughter and her Beagle? A few other points of interest might be where you found this and why did you bring it back here? Oh wait, you can skip the why you brought it home; you're Cassandra and you always bring home stray animals so there's that answer. Now, before I lose the control I am doing so well to hold onto, start spilling everything. Now!"

Carolyn's voice, at first rather calm considering the circumstances, had begun to climb in both pitch and volume. It was a good thing that their home was set away from the town and any other houses or the first interaction between human mother and baby dragon might have become a spectator event. But Cassie stood her ground.

"Mom, I know this is rather unusual but what a chance! Who else has ever had a dragon move in with them?"

"Back that up a bit. Who else has even seen a dragon?" Her mother was breathing rather deeply and obviously exerting a lot of effort to maintain her calm.

While human mother and daughter went back and forth about Bridget, Bea and her new baby continued to sniff each other. Between exploratory bouts of full body nosing, Bea would lick at stray bits of afterbirth. Bridget nuzzled her new mother and made contented grunting sounds. They seemed to be oblivious to the verbal battle raging around them.

Carolyn, realizing that her hard-headed daughter was not likely to back down quickly decided to try something else. "Cassie, let's go in and eat breakfast. We can discuss this afterwards. Bea and the dragon can stay out here until then."

You might think that Carolyn seemed awfully calm for someone who had just seen a small dragon; much less one whose daughter brought it home like a foundling rabbit, but you must remember that her mother had been someone who expected the odd and unusual. Her mother, Grand Mary, had suspected that Nature had more to show than what most people saw or even wanted to see. She had taught her daughter this lesson so when the dragon showed up outside her own door Carolyn wasn't so much shocked as surprised it hadn't arrived earlier. While that made it easier to accept that there really were such things as dragons it still didn't seem like such a great idea that her daughter brought it home.

Cassie relented. Like most people who have spent a lot of time around animals she knew that if she let her mother get to know the dragon then the possibility of it staying was high. After all, who can resist a puppy or kitten? So this baby had scales or something similar and not fur, it was still a baby with all the baby magic to make adults relent. And that's exactly what happened.

They went inside and ate. Afterwards Cassie and Carolyn came out to renew the discussion. But what Carolyn had not bargained for was the sight of Beatrice and Bridget curled up together on Bea's outside bed. The two of them nestled together in the over-sized blue bed that sat on the back porch. The morning light bounced off the silver body as it lay half covered by Bea. The two seemed to even breathe in tandem.

Maybe Carolyn let Bridget stay because for the first time since Grand Mary's death Cassie smiled so that her dimples showed again. Maybe Carolyn let the dragon stay because she made Beatrice forget her dead puppy. Or maybe she let the dragon baby stay because she was too cute to turn away. Who knows? Whatever turned the tide in Bridget's favor; she joined the family and in her own way, made the family more than what it had been before. But we'll get to that soon.

The war was won but there were many small battles yet to come. Where would the dragon live? Could it come inside? What should they feed it? Was it male or female? Who could know about it? So many questions but you won't learn about those now. That's for another time.

What is important to know is that Bridget stayed with Cassie and Bea. That one act of kindness changed all their lives.

Let's jump ahead a few weeks after the baby Bridget has doubled in length, and gained about forty pounds and, most importantly, knowledge of who she was.

It's a little known fact that as dragons grow their knowledge also grows. Oh, it's not like the rest of us where we learn from experience. We burn our fingers or read books or that sort of thing. No, dragons actually learn from other dragons' experiences. Everything other dragons have ever known seems to seep into the heads of growing dragons. So it was with Bridget.

Bridget grew in leaps and bounds. Sometimes her wings were three times as big as her body and later it would seem that her body had almost caught up. As quickly as she grew on the outside, her knowledge and ability to communicate with both Cassie and Beatrice increased even faster. She began to "remember" from the dragons who had come before her how to reach Cassie and Beatrice. She learned how to understand their thoughts and form her own thoughts to reach them. To reach Cassie, at first Bridget would form pictures and attach emotions. Beatrice thought in smells and tastes so Bridget began to reach out to her with thoughts laced with scents. Both girl and dog knew something was happening but it was Bea who was the first to realize the thoughts that didn't feel like they were hers came from her adopted dragon puppy.

The first thought that Bridget sent Bea was one of love, warm smells of their shared beds mixed with the taste of shared food (Bridget was eating out of Bea's plate). Bea, having always wanted to share thoughts with her adored Cassie, was elated. Sure, she could share thoughts with other dogs but this was her own adopted dragon puppy, a baby born of an egg but close enough to her to have come from her own womb. She couldn't touch minds with Cassie but she was not alone anymore!

When Bea felt the touch on her mind, she perked up. It was evening and she and Bridget had curled up together on their huge, soft bed in Cassie's room. Yes, Carolyn had relented to allow the young dragon into the house until she got a bit larger but Cassandra knew the dragon would have to move out to the barn soon. Neither Cassie not Carolyn knew that Bridget was a fire-breathing dragon or they might have never let her in the house at all. Fortunately, Bridget wasn't to develop that part of her legacy until months later.

Bea nuzzled Bridget's chin and pushed her head up so the dragon could look in her Hazel eyes. As their eyes met, Bea and Bridget felt the connection strengthen. Bea licked her adopted daughter's muzzle and eyes then both laid their heads back down and fell asleep.

A few days later, Cassie felt what she would soon realize was Bridget's touch on her mind. She was sitting on the veranda late in the afternoon, reading a book when she felt a slight tingling at the front of her head. It was like someone was running their fingers across the inside of her head. At the same time, Cassie saw and felt a thought that seemed to come from elsewhere. It looked like she was seeing her home from a different angle. Cassie looked around to see who might be close enough to be looking at her home. She reached out her right hand and grasped the soda can sitting there, brought it up to her lips, closed her eyes and took a long drink from it.

When Cassie opened her eyes, Bridget stood before her, bright blue eyes staring into hers. Bea sat a foot behind the young dragon allowing her girl and dragon to have a moment alone. Bea yawned, stretched her front legs and gave Cassie a Beagle grin. Bea's Hazel eyes held some secret as she too stared up at her girl.

"Was that you?" Cassie knew the dragon couldn't speak but who else could be trying to reach her this way? She directed her question to the luminescent dragon. Glancing from Bridget, then to Bea and back again, Cassandra felt the hairs on the back of her neck start to tingle and rise.

Cassie sat the soda down, placed a small magnetic book mark with the comic face of a brown dog on the page she had stopped reading and set the book down on the brown wicker side table to her left. Her neck was tingling even more and the fingers inside the top of her skull had begun a

179

finger tap dance. By now the picture in her mind was even clearer.

She was seeing herself through the dragon's eyes.

And then Bridget spoke. I know I said that most dragons don't speak human language but Bridget wasn't just any dragon. Bridget was the last dragon. Bridget had all the knowledge of all other dragons, including human language. And she so wanted to speak to her girl.

"Casssssandra." Her snake-like tongue held onto the "s" in Cassie's name and snapped it like a whip.

It was a good thing that Cassie was still sitting down or she might have fallen down as her knees became unbaked clay.

"Cassssandra, I want to talk. May I talk to you?"

What could Cassie say? She had always wanted to actually talk with another species and here was her chance. Maybe if she had been older and more cautious, she might have run away. Maybe if Cassie had been younger and more easily frightened she might have run away. But Cassie, the girl who was betwixt and between, sat on her porch listening to the last dragon in the world call her name.

And what did the last dragon say to the only girl who might have listened to her? Many, many things. But the one thing that Cassie heard of all the things Bridget said to her that day was that the dragon could tell her not just what she knew; Bridget could act a translator between Bea and Cassie. Bea had always understood most of what Cassie said but now Cassie could be even closer to her beloved Beagle. Bridget could speak for Beatrice.

The three of them sat together on the veranda as the sun set, sharing all the things they had wanted to say to each other.

Bridget, the ancient baby, joined the three – girl, dog and dragon – into something more than the sum of their parts. Bridget was no longer the only one; she would never know her own dragon mother but she had Bea and Cassie who would love her until the end of their days. Beatrice still mourned her dead puppy but the excitement of her scaled daughter and being able to actually pass her thoughts to her human helped her look forward to the next day. And Cassandra could live her dream. With Bridget's help she could learn from Bea and even other animals.

Cassandra was no longer betwixt and between, alone. Cassie, Bea and Bridget had each other.

Nature is cruel and moves on Her way with seemingly little care for humans, dogs and even dragons. Grandmothers die and puppies are stillborn. Dragon babies are born thousands of years after all the rest of their kind are gone.

But sometimes Nature smiles.

Mike Resnick is a a literary master and this story is a supreme example of his talent. It won the American Dog Writers Award in 1977. It appeared in Hunting Dog Magazine. Fair warning—get the tissues out right now before proceeding.

The Last Dog

by Mike Resnick

The Dog—old, mangy, his vertebrae forming little ridges beneath the slack skin that covered his gaunt body—trotted through the deserted streets, nose to the ground. He was missing half an ear and most of his tail, and caked blood covered his neck like a scarf. He may have been gold once, or light brown, but now he looked like an old red brick, even down to the straw and mud that clung to those few portions of his body which still retained any hair at all.

Since he had no true perception of the passage of time, he had no idea when he had last eaten—except that it had been a long time ago. A broken radiator in an automobile graveyard had provided water for the past week, and kept him in the area long after the last of the rusty, translucent liquid was gone.

He was panting now, his breath coming in a never-ending series of short spurts and gasps. His sides ached, his eyes watered, and every now and then he would trip over the rubble of the decayed and ruined buildings that lined the tortuously fragmented street. The toes of his feet were covered by sores and calluses, and both his dew claws had long since been torn off.

He continued trotting, occasionally shivering from the cold breeze that whistled down the streets of the lifeless city. Once he saw a rat, but a premature whine of hunger had sent it scurrying off into the debris before he could catch it, and so he trotted, his stride a little shorter, his chest hurting a little more, searching for sustenance so that he would live another day to hunt again and eat again and live still another day.

Then suddenly he froze, his mud-caked nostrils testing the wind, the pitiful stump of a tail held rigidly behind him. He remained motionless for almost a minute, except for a spasmodic quivering in one foreleg, then slunk into the shadows and advanced silently down the street.

He emerged at what had once been an intersection, stared at the thing across the street from him, and blinked. His eyesight, none too good even in the days of his youth and health, was insufficient to the task, and so he inched forward, belly to ground, flecks of saliva falling onto his chest.

The Man heard a faint shuffling sound and looked into the shadows, a segment of an old two-by-four in his hand. He, too, was gaunt and dirty, his hair unkempt, four teeth missing and another one half rotted away. His feet were wrapped in old rags, and the only thing that held his clothes together was the dirt.

"Who's there?" he said in a rasping voice.

The Dog, fangs bared, moved out from between buildings and began advancing, a low growl rumbling in his throat.

The Man turned to face him, strengthening his grip on his makeshift warclub. They stopped when they were fifteen feet apart, tense and unmoving. Slowly the Man raised his club to striking position; slowly the Dog gathered his hind legs beneath him.

Then, without warning, a rat raced out of the debris and ran between them. Savage cries escaped the lips of both the Dog and the Man. The Dog pounced, but the Man's stick was even faster; it flew through the air and landed on the rat's back, pulping it to the ground and killing it instantly.

The Man walked forward to retrieve his weapon and his prey. As he reached down, the Dog emitted a low growl. The Man stared at him for a long moment; then, very slowly, very carefully, he picked up one end of the stick. He sawed with the other end against the smashed body of the rat until it split in half, and shoved one pulpy segment toward the Dog. The Dog remained motionless for a few seconds, then lowered his head, grabbed the blood-spattered piece of flesh and tissue, and raced off across the street with it. He stopped at the edge of the shadows, lay down, and began gnawing at his grisly meal. The Man watched him for a moment, then picked up his half of the rat, squatted down like some million-years-gone progenitor, and did the same.

When his meal was done the Man belched once, walked over to the still-standing wall of a building, sat with his back against it, laid his two-by-four across his thighs, and stared at the Dog. The Dog, licking forepaws that would never again be clean, stared back.

They slept thus, motionless, in the ghost city. When the Man awoke the next morning he arose, and the Dog did likewise. The Man balanced his stick across his shoulder and began walking, and after a moment the Dog followed him. The Man spent most of the day walking through the city, looking into the soft innards of stores and shops, occasionally cursing as dead store after dead store refused to yield up shoes, or coats, or food. At twilight he built a small fire in the rubble and looked around for the Dog, but could not find it.

The man slept uneasily and awoke some two hours before sunrise. The Dog was sleeping about twenty feet away from him. The Man sat up abruptly, and the Dog, startled, raced off. Ten minutes later he was back, stopping about eighty feet distant, ready to race away again at an instant's warning, but back nonetheless.

The Man looked at the Dog, shrugged, and began walking in a northerly direction. By midday he had reached the outskirts of the city and, finding the ground soft and muddy, he dug a hole with his hands and his stick. He sat down next to it and waited as water slowly seeped into it. Finally he reached his hands down, cupping them together, and drew the precious fluid up to his lips. He did this twice more, then began walking again. Some instinct prompted him to turn back, and he saw the Dog eagerly lapping up what water remained.

He made another kill that night, a medium-sized bird that had flown into the second-floor room of a crumbling hotel and couldn't remember how to fly out before he pulped it. He ate most of it, put the rest into what remained of a pocket, and walked outside. He threw it on the ground and the Dog slunk out of the shadows, still tense but no longer growling. The Man sighed, returned to the hotel, and climbed up to the second floor. There were no rooms with windows intact, but he did find one with half a mattress remaining, and he collapsed upon it.

When he awoke, the Dog was lying in the doorway, sleeping soundly.

They walked, a little closer this time, through the remains of the forest that was north of the city. After they had proceeded about a dozen miles they found a small stream that was not quite dry and drank from it, the Man first and then the Dog. That night the man lit another fire and the Dog lay down on the opposite side of it. The next day the Dog killed a small, undernourished squirrel. He did not share it with the Man, but neither did he growl or bare his teeth as the Man approached. That night the Man killed an opossum, and they remained in the area for two days, until the last of the marsupial's flesh had been consumed.

They walked north for almost two weeks, making an occasional kill, finding an occasional source of water. Then one night it rained, and there was no fire, and the Man sat, arms hugging himself, beneath a large tree. Soon the Dog approached him, sat about four feet away, and then slowly, ever so slowly, inched forward as the rain struck his flanks. The Man reached out absently and stroked the Dog's neck. It was their first physical contact, and the Dog leaped back, snarling. The Man withdrew his hand and sat motionless, and soon the Dog moved forward again.

After a period of time that might have been ten minutes or perhaps two hours, the Man reached out once more, and this time, although the Dog trembled and tensed, he did not pull away. The Man's long fingers slowly moved up the sore-covered neck, scratched behind the torn ears, gently stroked the scarred head. Finally the Man withdrew his hand and rolled over on his side. The Dog looked at him for a moment, then sighed and laid up against his emaciated body.

The Man awoke the next morning to the feeling of something warm and scaly pressed into his hand. It was not the cool, moist nose of the dogs of literature, because this was not a dog of literature. This was the Last Dog, and he was the Last Man, and if they looked less than heroic, at least there was no one around to see and bemoan how the mighty had fallen.

The Man patted the Dog's head, arose, stretched, and began walking. The Dog trotted at his side, and for the first time in many years the nub of his tail moved rapidly from side to side. They hunted and ate and drank and slept, then repeated the procedure again and again.

And then they came to the Other.

The Other looked like neither Man nor Dog, nor like anything else of earth, as indeed it was not. It had come from beyond Centauri, beyond Arcturus, past Antares. from deep at the core of the galaxy, where the stars pressed so close together that nightfall never came. It had come, and had seen, and had conquered.

"You!" hissed the Man, holding his stick at the ready.

"You are the last," said the Other. "For six years I have scoured and scourged the face of this planet, for six years I have eaten alone and slept alone and lived alone and hunted down the survivors of the war one by one, and you are the last. There is only you to be slain, and then I may go home."

And, so saying, it withdrew a weapon that looked strangely like a pistol, but wasn't.

The Man crouched and prepared to hurl his stick, but even as he did so a brick-red, scarred, bristling engine of destruction hurtled past him, leaping through space for the Other. The Other touched what passed for a belt, made a quick gesture in the air, and the Dog bounced back off of something that was invisible, unsensible, but tangible.

Then, very slowly, almost casually, the Other pointed its weapon at the Man. There was no explosion, no flash of light, no whirring of gears, but suddenly the Man grasped his throat and fell to the ground.

The Dog got up and limped painfully over to the Man. He nuzzled his face, whined once, and pawed at his body, trying to turn it over.

"It is no use," said the Other, although its lips no longer moved. "He was the last, and now he is dead."

The Dog whined again, and pushed the Man's lifeless head with his muzzle.

"Come, Animal," said the Other wordlessly. "Come with me and I shall feed you and tend to your wounds."

I will stay with the Man, said the Dog, also wordlessly.

"But he is dead," said the Other. "Soon you will grow hungry and weak."

I was hungry and weak before, said the Dog.

The Other took a step forward, but stopped as the Dog bared his teeth and growled.

"He was not worth your loyalty," said the Other.

He was my—The Dog's brain searched for a word, but the concept it sought was complex far beyond its meager abilities to formulate. *He was my friend.*

"He was my enemy," said the Other. "He was petty and barbarous and unscrupulous and all that is worst in a sentient being. He was Man."

Yes, said the Dog. *He was Man.* With another whimper, he lay down beside the body of the Man and rested his head on its chest.

"There are no more," said the Other. "And soon you will leave him."

The Dog looked up at the Other and snarled again, and then the Other was gone and the Dog was alone with the Man. He licked him and nuzzled him and stood guard over him for two days and two nights, and then, as the Other had said he would, he left to hunt for food and water.

And he came to a valley of fat, lazy rabbits and cool, clear ponds, and he ate and drank and grew strong, and his wounds began to scab over and heal, and his coat grew long and luxuriant.

And because he was only a Dog, it was not too long before he forgot that there had ever been such a thing as a Man, except on those chilly nights when he lay alone beneath a tree in the valley and dreamt of a bond that had been forged by a gentle touch upon the head or a soft word barely audible above the crackling of a small fire.

And, being a Dog, one day he forgot even that, and assumed that the emptiness within him came only from hunger. And when he grew old and feeble and sick, he did not seek out the Man's barren bones and lie down to die beside them, but rather he dug a hole in the damp earth near the pond and lay there, his eyes half closed, a numbness setting in at his extremities and working its way slowly toward his heart.

And just before the Dog exhaled his last breath, he felt a moment of panic. He tried to jump up, but found that he couldn't. He whimpered once, his eyes clouding over with fear and something else; and then it seemed to him that a bony, gentle hand was caressing his ears, and, with a single wag of his tail, the Last Dog closed his eyes for the last time and prepared to join a God of stubbled beard and torn clothes and feet wrapped in rags.

www.ingramcontent.com/pod-product-compliance
Lightning Source LLC
Chambersburg PA
CBHW060939180626

46817CB00004B/1630